CROWNLESS

FORGOTTEN QUEER HISTORIES OF IMPERIAL ROME

To Paola,
to a friend, whose insight, generosity and
ability to truly listen I deeply admire.
With gratitude and affection

by

J. H. M. CARLISLE

CROWNLESS

Published by Rondanini Publishing™ Ltd
www.rondanini.com

Suite 6438, Unit 3A,
34-35 Hatton Garden,
Holborn,
London,
EC1N 8DX

ISBN: 978-1-918177-00-8
eISBN: 978-1-918177-01-5

First Edition: August 2025

Cover and interior design by Rondanini Publishing™ Ltd

Printed in the United Kingdom

To the queers in history—

To the queers in history: erased, rewritten, criminalised. Yet still enduring.

This book is for you.

"Some say a host of horsemen is the most beautiful thing on the dark earth. I say it is whatever one loves."

— **Sappho of Lesbos**, c. 630 BCE.

May your echoes become voices, your shadows stories, and you be remembered—not as ornaments of empire, but as souls who endured it.

TABLE OF CONTENTS

SPORUS

The Boy Who Became Memory

PROLOGUE

They called me by a name that was never mine.

Sporus—a joke, a wound, a title that meant "seed without fruit." They gave it to me the day they decided I would become someone else, when they looked at my face and saw not a person but a possibility.

I write this knowing no one will read it. The dead empress, whose image I carry, has temples, coins, and poets singing her praises. I have only these words, scratched in secret and hidden where archaeologists might find them centuries hence.

If they do, let them know: the boy from Bithynia was real.

Before I was Sporus—before I was made to resemble her, before emperors fought over the right to possess my transformed flesh—I was Aeneas.

I pressed olives with my father. I had a brother who made me laugh. I held a wooden cup carved from a tree older than the empire.

I want someone to know this: I was human first.

What they made me into came after.

But it never replaced what came before.

CHAPTER 1:

A BOY FROM BITHYNIA

"The Empire's appetite is infinite, but it prefers to feed on the young."

— Seneca the Younger

Bithynia — 64 CE

The olive press groaned like a dying thing. I had known its voice longer than my own.

Most mornings, it was just background. But today, it was louder. Older. Heavier. Or maybe I was simply hearing it differently.

Father and I worked in rhythm. He gripped the wooden lever and leaned his full weight into it while I ladled the thick, green-gold oil into amphorae. Sunlight slanted through the workshop's open wall, and the oil glowed as it fell. I watched the shimmer, imagining it was honey—or light made liquid.

"Aeneas," my father said. Not sharply, but enough. He did not look up.

I blinked and returned to the task. My hands knew the steps: ladle, pour, wipe the lip. Every drop mattered. Waste was theft—he had said it since I was little. Theft from the family, from the gods, from the future. That future had always been vague, distant, something for other people. I never asked what he meant. Some truths you did not press.

His hands moved over mine as we sealed the amphora with wax and pine resin. Brown hands, calloused and cracked from years of this exact labour. My hands looked different. Too smooth. Too slender. Sometimes I stared at them and wondered about my purpose—or if I had simply never learned how to be what this place required.

"You have your mother's hands," he said, as always. "Soft. Meant for finer things."

I once asked whether that was acceptable. He did not answer.

When I was younger, I would sit beside the press and dream of other lives: a merchant in Nicomedia, a charioteer, a poet with a laurel crown. I used to draw letters in the oil dust. My mother would wipe them away before Father saw.

Lately, the dreams came less often. The oil stained, the press groaned, the sun rose and fell. The rhythm of the groove had become the rhythm of me.

Until the dust appeared on the road.

"Riders!" my mother called, her voice clipped. She stood in the doorway, shielding her eyes. "From the city."

I stepped beside her. The road shimmered with heat, but even blurred by distance, the silhouettes were unmistakable: three men, mounted and moving fast. Not locals. Too upright. Too clean. They rode as if they owned the road.

Father set down his tools, as if buying time. His mouth tightened.

"Keep working," he said, almost gently.

But no one moved. Not really. When Rome sent riders, you did not press more olives. You held your breath.

The men arrived in a spray of dust. The lead rider dismounted in one fluid motion. Tall, lean, dressed for business—not for battle, but with the same arrogance. He unrolled a wax tablet and read before introducing himself, as though he needed the reminder.

"Marcus Junius Calvus," he said. "Tax collector for this district."

Father wipes his hands on his tunic. "Gaius Aenius Fortunatus. My property is current."

"That's the issue," Calvus replies. "Your taxes are current based on last year's values. But under the provincial reassessment order, land prices in this corridor have risen substantially."

He gestures toward our grove, as though it has already been priced, measured, and conquered.

Father frowns. "We haven't added acreage. Our yield hasn't changed."

"But the road has," Calvus says, smiling. "And roads improve access. Access raises value. Value raises tax obligations. Sixty per cent."

The number lands like a slap. My mother lets out a small sound. Father says nothing.

Calvus taps the tablet. "You'll find the reassessment consistent with neighbouring properties. The good news is—we're not here to confiscate. The Empire understands the pressures of provincial life."

Behind him, one of the other men chuckles.

What follows is almost theatrical. Calvus offers a loan: twenty per cent interest. Father baulks. Calvus feigns sympathy. Suggests alternatives.

The trap is already closed.

"Indenture," he says finally. "Seven years. One son. Preferably, the elder, for maturity. Good looks help."

He doesn't say it brutally, just as a fact.

Father stiffens. "My son is not for sale."

"Of course not," Calvus replies smoothly. "It's not slavery. He'll serve in a senator's household—in Rome. A noble family: Gaius Petronius. Cultured. Influential. The boy will be educated, clothed, and safe. The debt was resolved. He will return home a man."

His tone is honeyed. His eyes are not.

My mother's hand finds my wrist, her grip iron.

Calvus shrugs. "Or we initiate seizure proceedings. The land becomes state property. The family relocates—if they can find a place not blacklisted for unpaid taxes. The debt will follow. It always does."

My father stares at the ground. My chest tightens.

He doesn't look at me. That's what tells me it's done.

The bond is a small thing: a tablet, a seal, two names. Calvus adds fees—travel, preparation, and administrative overhead. The sum balloons, but he assures us the labour exchange remains the same: seven years.

Preparation begins immediately.

I don't remember much of the rest of the day. My mother packs things into a cloth bag. My father stands beside the press but doesn't touch it. The oil is still warm from our morning work, cooling into stillness.

That night, we sat together on the floor. The table feels too formal, too ordinary for what has changed.

No one eats. There's bread, cheese, and wine, but it's all spectacle.

"Seven years," my father says at last. "You'll return with knowledge, a trade, and connections. This is not an end."

"It's Rome," my mother murmurs. "When they take something, they don't return it."

She covers her mouth as if the words have slipped out.

Father takes her hand. "He'll come back."

We all pretend to believe him.

Later, I lie awake on my straw mattress, the summer air thick with the smell of olives, dust, and something I cannot name. My brother sleeps beside me, curled like a child though he is grown. My mother hums in the other room—a song without a melody.

I reach beneath my mattress and pull out the wooden cup my father carved when I was small. Simple olive wood, smoothed by years of use. He shaped it to fit my fingers and told me the tree had stood longer than the Empire.

He said its wood would outlast stone.

I whisper into it: “Aeneas. Aeneas of Bithynia.”

The name feels thinner than it once did—like something that could be rubbed away.

I think about what Calvus said: “Safe.” “Respected.” “Not slavery.”

But I have seen men walk the road to Nicomedia in chains. I have seen boys—softer, prettier than me—vanish into Roman villas and never return.

I try to imagine the city, Rome: marble and gold, voices like thunder.

But what I feel is the weight of hands I have not yet met, the gaze of men who will not ask my name.

Sleep takes its time. When it comes, it brings no peace. I dream of roads that wind forever, oil that spills without end, and voices calling me by names I do not recognise.

Tomorrow, I leave the grove. Tomorrow, I leave the boy I have always been.

The agreement says seven years.

But part of me already knows: in Rome, time doesn’t run straight. And names don’t come back.

CHAPTER 2:

THE SENATOR'S HOUSE

"In Rome, a slave's name is whatever his master calls him that day."

— Pliny the Elder

Rome — Summer, 64 CE

The city hits like a fever.

Not the heat—I'm used to heat—but the density. The way it presses in from every direction: people, noise, smells, stone. Everything is too much, too loud, too fast. Rome doesn't move like a city. It pulses like a living thing, and I'm inside its chest.

Our cart lurches past crowded stalls and bodies pressing close without touching. A child runs alongside for a few moments, begging in broken Latin. A man with no legs drags himself through garbage near a fountain carved with lions. I try not to stare.

"Stay alert," Brutus grunts from the driver's bench. He doesn't turn around. "Boys from the provinces disappear in Rome. Fast."

Lucius sits beside me, face unreadable. Marcus hides behind the cart's edge, trying not to breathe the stench—dung, sweat, rotting fish, and something metallic that might be blood.

I keep my hands folded in my lap and force myself to watch.

I want to see everything, because nothing will ever be familiar again, and I want to remember what it feels like at the edge.

The buildings grow taller the farther in we go. At home, three stories meant wealth. Here, they stack six high, leaning out over the streets like giants listening to gossip. Between them, I glimpse banners fluttering with symbols I don't recognise, inscriptions I can barely read. Latin, Greek, something else. All languages spoken at once—none of them mine.

Aeneas of Bithynia. Still my name, but already fading behind my teeth.

We turn onto a wide avenue paved in white stone, suddenly clear of the chaos. The noise drops. The people are richer, the walls higher, the air somehow cleaner. Green gardens flash behind iron gates.

"The Palatine," Brutus says. His tone changes when he says it—like a prayer or a warning.

Ahead, the gates of bronze gleam in the sun. Two guards wait with polished armour and dead eyes. As we approach, one checks a scroll while the other peers into the cart as if choosing meat at a market.

"Petronius' household," Brutus says.

The gates open.

We pass through.

Inside, everything is wrong in a different way. The chaos of the city gives way to too much order, too much silence. The courtyard is lined with marble. Statues are everywhere—gods, men, creatures with wings. A fountain sends thin streams into a pool so clear it reflects the sky better than the sky itself.

We stop in the shadow of the main portico. I climb down, legs stiff, mouth dry.

"Stand straight," Brutus says quietly, not unkindly. "You'll want to look useful."

A woman appears before we've even fully dismounted.

Tall, pale-skinned, perhaps forty. Her stola flows like water. Her hair is sculpted into careful coils, each one more expensive than our farm.

She walks as though the space belongs to her.

"Domina Volumnia," Brutus says, bowing. "The new arrivals. Three boys from Bithynia."

She looks at Lucius. "Good height. Sturdy."

Then Marcus. "Still growing."

And then me.

Her eyes linger. Not long—but long enough.

"This one is exceptional," she says softly. "My husband will be very pleased."

She doesn't smile. She doesn't need to.

We're led to a bathing chamber. Not for comfort—for display.

The water is warm, scented with something sharp and floral. Two men bathe us with clinical efficiency. They scrape our skin with curved blades, trim our hair, and oil our bodies until we shine like statues. My clothes are taken, replaced with a tunic softer than anything I've worn before. The sandals are lined with leather that feels like air.

"Why does everything fit?" Marcus whispers.

"Because they knew," Lucius mutters. "We weren't bought. We were ordered."

The words sit in my stomach like stones—heavy, settled.

A man named Alexios arrives to inspect us.

Greek, perhaps fifty, with silver streaks in his beard and sharp eyes that miss nothing. He looks more like a tutor than a servant, but when he speaks, everyone listens.

"You'll follow instructions precisely," he says. "Speak only when addressed. Keep your eyes down unless ordered otherwise. You are not here to impress—you are here to serve."

His gaze lingers on me a half-second longer than on the others. Something flickers across his face. No recognition. Not yet. But attention.

"You will be assigned based on aptitude," he continues. "Some of you will clean. Some will serve. Some will learn to entertain. All roles are necessary. None is safe."

That last part isn't in the rules. It's in his voice.

We are led through corridors painted with scenes of gods and battles. Not real ones—idealised. A world without dirt, without fear. A lie wrapped in gold.

I try not to look too closely. I don't want to learn to admire it.

We're given a shared room: three beds, three chests, a single window with a narrow slice of sky. It's cleaner and richer than our entire house in Bithynia.

I sit on the bed but don't lie down. My body no longer understands softness.

Marcus finally breaks the silence. "How long do you think it will be before we're allowed to write home?"

Alexios had mentioned correspondence on feast days, with permission. But none of us believes that now.

Lucius answers in silence. That is louder than anything else.

Later, we are brought to the atrium to meet the senator.

It is a hall meant for theatre. The ceiling opens to the sky, and a shallow pool reflects the painted walls like a mirror. Marble busts of ancestors line the edges, their eyes blank and eternal.

Senator Petronius enters without ceremony. His toga flows perfectly. He walks like a man born knowing power belongs to him.

He does not shout. He does not need to.

He walks straight to us and stops in front of me.

"This one?" he asks.

"Yes, Senator," says Volumnia behind him. "Remarkable resemblance."

He studies my face as if it were art, not in admiration, but in calculation.

"What is your name?"

I answer the way Alexios taught us. "This slave is called Aeneas, Senator."

He smiles faintly. "Appropriate."

That is all.

He turns to Alexios. "Begin with general training. No outside contact. I want full integration."

Alexios nods. "Understood."

And just like that, I am inside the machine.

That night, I lie awake while the others sleep.

I stare at the ceiling, frescoes of men riding chariots across the sky, immortal and perfect. There is no room here for boys from olive groves.

I reach into the chest at the foot of my bed and find my one possession: the wooden cup.

Tonight, I am not whispering into it. I only hold it, my mouth too dry for prayers.

Today, I crossed into a place where names are costumes and bodies are tools, and someone, somewhere, has already decided how mine will be used.

But I am still here. Still me, however fragile that might be.

And I am watching.

CHAPTER 3:

GLIMPSES OF POWER

"The palace shows you wonders so you forget to ask the price of admission."

— Court graffiti, Palatine Hill

Rome — Autumn, 64 CE

The summons arrives at dawn.

Not with shouting or ceremony, but with a folded tablet pressed into Alexios's hand by a man in imperial livery, his cloak edged in purple and his expression too still to be casual.

Senator Petronius reads it once and says only:

"The emperor requests our presence at a private gathering."

No one moves.

"Tomorrow evening," he adds. "Informal."

The word carries weight. Nothing involving emperors is informal.

The day becomes a quiet storm.

Volumnia oversees preparations like a general—inspecting gifts, sending messengers, dictating arrangements. Silver goblets etched with mythological scenes are polished. A bronze statuette of Apollo is boxed and wrapped in dyed linen. She selects perfumes from a chest that smells like Arabia itself.

Meanwhile, Alexios prepares us.

"You three," he says—me, Lucius, Marcus. "You'll serve wine. Pour only when asked. Do not speak unless spoken to. The emperor's eye wanders. Do not draw it without cause."

He looks at me last.

"Especially you."

I nod, though I don't understand. Not fully.

But I will.

The bath is hotter than usual. My skin flushes as they scrub me raw, then rub oil into my limbs until I gleam. My nails are cleaned and shaped. My hair is curled slightly, pinned with a single bronze clasp. I look like someone I don't know.

The tunic they gave me is white silk, nearly sheer. The sandals fasten with delicate bronze wire. Everything fits as if I'd been measured long before I arrived.

"Eyes down," Alexios reminds us as we line up. "You are not the show. You are the setting."

Rome at night breathes differently. The streets are quieter, but never still. Music drifts from behind closed doors. Laughter, too—though hushed. There's always a shadow behind the sound, a question behind every joy.

The Palatine glows with torchlight. The emperor's palace—unfinished, yet sprawling—feels like a living thing, hungry and always growing. We enter through side passages, where other servants move like ghosts. No one speaks above a whisper.

Inside, the world changes.

The hall is round, high-ceilinged, and painted like the night sky. Stars move above us—literally move—driven by mechanisms I cannot see. Tables stand in concentric circles around a central platform. Food glistens on trays. Wine catches the light like blood.

Statues of the emperor in divine form decorate every wall: Apollo, Dionysus, Jupiter. Nero's face on each of them.

I avoid gazing for too long. They seem to eye us back.

"Magnificent, isn't it?"

The voice startles me. A woman steps from behind a column—golden-haired, draped in soft green silk. Her smile is precise, her gaze cutting.

I've heard her name whispered, though never directly. The former empress. The dead one.

"The new acquisitions?" she asks Alexios, though her eyes remain on me.

"From Bithynia," Alexios answers. "Senator Petronius's latest patronage"

She circles us slowly, then stops when she reaches me.

"This one is remarkable," she says. "The bone structure. The resemblance."

Her fingers hover near my cheek, not quite touching.

"They say her final moments were..." She pauses, considering. "Violent. They whispered that the marble floor cracked beneath her head when she fell."

The image settles cold in my stomach—a preview of what breaking looks like.

"Yes, Domina," Alexios says carefully.

She doesn't answer. She just looks at me, and something in that look says: I see what you are. I see what you're for.

Then she walks away.

The room fills slowly with guests—senators, their wives, clients, merchants—all glittering, all dangerous. Each arrival is announced, and every placement at a table is a message.

I keep my head down and my hands ready. I refill cups, arrange pillows, and retrieve a dropped fig. It's a rhythm. I can live in rhythm.

Until the emperor arrives.

No trumpets. No speech. Just presence.

He enters like someone who expects the world to rearrange itself around him—and it does. Nero is younger than I expected. His face is broad, his lips full, his curls artfully dishevelled. His eyes are the problem. They're too alive. Not kind. Not cruel. Just always watching.

He moves to his place. The room leans toward him like flowers to the sun.

"Tonight," he says, "we celebrate beauty. The kind that whispers, that pierces, that endures."

Everyone laughs. Then stops.

Dinner begins.

We serve.

The food is extravagant—birds wrapped inside birds, gold-dusted fruits, cheeses shaped like stars. The wine is sweeter than anything I've ever smelled.

I move as I've been trained: fluid, silent.

Then I feel it.

A gaze.

I look up.

Nero sees me.

His eyes don't move when mine meet his. He leans toward the golden-haired woman and says something I can't hear. She smiles without looking.

I glance away and spill wine down my wrist.

Alexios is suddenly beside me. "Steady," he whispers. "You're not here to drink it."

I nod. Try again.

The room blurs after that. I serve automatically, barely tasting the air.

At some point, I feel him again.

"You," the emperor says.

I freeze.

"The boy with the wine. Come here."

I move. The whole room watches.

I stop a few paces from him and bow my head.

"Closer," he says.

I obey.

"What's your name?"

"This slave is called Aeneas, Caesar."

He laughs softly. "Aeneas. A Trojan hero. A founder. How poetic."

He studies me—not like a man studies a man, but like an artist studies clay.

His fingers, warm and dry, lift my chin.

"Remarkable," he murmurs. "The likeness is almost divine."

To what, I don't ask.

He turns to Petronius. "Your taste improves each season."

Petronius, standing nearby, bows slightly. "Your praise honours me, Caesar."

Nero's hand falls away.

"You may return," he says to me. "But remember: the gods notice beauty. And so do emperors."

I back away. Don't run. Don't stumble.

At my station, Marcus stares at me, eyes wide. Lucius won't look at all.

The meal continues, but nothing feels the same.

I've been seen.

Later, as guests leave and laughter softens into whispers, the golden-haired woman approaches again.

She stops in front of me and tilts her head.

"The emperor was very taken with you," she says.

I say nothing.

She reaches out—just a fingertip against my collarbone.

"You should understand what you are now," she says softly. "A mirror. A memory. A resemblance too perfect to ignore."

I want to ask, Resemblance to whom?

But I already know the answer.

She walks away.

Back in the senator's house, we undress in silence. I place my tunic gently in the chest and fold the sandals like relics.

I lie in bed, face to the ceiling, unmoving.

My chest feels hollow.

I was nothing this morning. A servant. A shadow.

Now I'm something.

And I don't know what it is, or who will own it.

I hold the wooden cup and stare at it, unblinking.

I don't whisper tonight.

Because the name in my mouth is still mine.

But I don't know how much longer that will be true.

CHAPTER 4:

BEHIND THE THRONE

"Beauty is the cruellest currency—it spends itself in the earning."

— Ovid, Metamorphoses

The Palace of Nero — Winter, 64-65 CE

The second summons comes without warning. No messenger this time, only Alexios at my door before sunrise.

"Dress quickly," he says. "No food. The emperor has requested your presence."

No explanation. No hint of tone.

My hands shake slightly as I fasten the tunic. The fabric still smells of olive oil from the last washing. I don't know if that's comforting or dangerous.

As I follow Alexios through the villa and into the city, I try to steady my breath.

Requested. Not demanded.

But I'm learning that in Rome, words rarely mean what they sound like.

We enter through the eastern service wing of the palace. It's quieter here: no banquet tables, no gilded ceremony halls—just long corridors lit by steady torches and watched by silent guards. The walls are less adorned. More stone than spectacle.

I expected gold. I find order.

The air changes as we move deeper—colder, tighter. As if the building itself wants to keep us inside.

Alexios doesn't speak. He walks like he's done this many times. I try to match his steps, stay silent, and look like someone who knows how to obey without effort.

Inside a private chamber, we're met by a man in a dark cloak, not much older than me. His expression is unreadable, but he speaks with quiet authority.

"You'll be shown to the imperial dressing rooms," he says. "You'll be observed. Do not speak unless instructed. Do not ask questions."

He opens a second door.

"Enter."

The room is smaller than I expected. Narrow. Bright.

There are mirrors—dozens—lined along the walls, full-length and angled, burnished bronze that reflects me from every direction. A handful of men in tunics move in slow, precise rhythms, adjusting fabric, testing cosmetics, murmuring in Greek and Latin.

They don't look at me as I step inside. Not at first.

But one by one, they begin to circle.

They touch my shoulders. Tilt my face. One adjusts my hair, tugging it slightly behind my ears. Another lifts my arm, examining the angle of my elbow as if measuring a sculpture.

Still no words.

Then Nero enters.

He doesn't walk—he arrives.

He is dressed simply: tunic, cloak, sandals. Yet everything is coordinated, an effortless, calculated contrast to the extravagance of his court.

He looks me over, then speaks to the stylists.

"Closer. Let me see the line of the jaw again."

One of the men tilts my chin upward.

"Yes," Nero says. "He'll do."

He circles me once, slowly. I keep my eyes forward—still, present, not challenging.

"You don't need to be afraid," he says.

I don't answer.

"You're part of something now," he continues. "A spectacle with purpose. The Empire needs beauty. Not just conquest, not just law, but embodiment. Memory."

He moves in front of me again. Our eyes meet.

"You resemble her."

He doesn't say who. But I know.

The dead empress. The one who fell. Whose skull split against marble.

"Do you understand what that means?" he asks.

"No, Caesar," I say honestly.

He smiles. "Good. Let it mean what I decide."

Over the next hour, they dress me in formal robes. Not women's clothing—yet—but close. The tunic is dyed rose, threaded with silver. My hair is styled upward. My hands are painted with perfumed oil. No one tells me why.

"You will appear at court functions," says a new voice—Vitellius, I learn. An advisor. Sharp, dry. "Not as a servant, but as a symbol. The emperor has decreed it."

He hands Alexios a scroll. "This contains a new protocol. Household restrictions. No further labour assignments. No contact with the senator's household unless approved in advance."

I glance at Alexios. His jaw tightens, just a fraction. He does not look at me.

That evening, I return to Petronius's estate—but not as a member of his staff.

I sleep in a separate chamber.

I eat alone.

No chores. No instructions. Just a folded garment laid out at sunrise, and a carriage waiting in the morning.

The next day, I return to the palace.

And the next.

And the next.

Each visit is different. Sometimes I stand in a receiving room beside a vase of white lilies. Sometimes I sit at the edge of the emperor's study while he dictates letters or composes poetry. Sometimes I walk behind him through the gardens as he describes a dream.

I begin to understand: I am not being trained. I am being recast.

At first, I tell myself it's survivable. Better this than the mines. Better this than the whip. Better to be visible, favoured.

But the more they adjust me—my posture, my tone, even the way I breathe when spoken to—the less certain I become.

I catch myself imitating Nero's speech rhythms. My smile begins to resemble that of the dead empress in the frescoes I've seen. I sit not like myself, but like someone remembered.

Even my silence begins to feel curated.

On the fifth visit, he gave me a ring.

It's delicate: bronze, with a carved agate inlay of a woman's face.

He doesn't say what it means. He doesn't have to.

"Wear it always," he says.

I do.

One afternoon, while the emperor rehearses a musical display for a private feast, he asks me to stand beside him while he sings.

He sings to me. Not at me—to me.

I don't know what to do with my face.

I try to admire. Softness. Openness.

Later, one of the stylists tells me I did well. "He likes the way your eyes fill with sorrow. It suits you."

I hadn't known they had.

That night, in the mirror, I study the lines of my face. The shape of my lips. The curve of my shoulders.

I still look like myself.

But only just.

Word reaches the Senator's house that I've been "elevated." Not in rank—slaves don't rise—but in visibility, in use.

Petronius congratulates himself. Volumnia doesn't mention me at all.

Lucius and Marcus avoid my eyes the one time our paths cross. I don't blame them. I wouldn't want to be seen with me either.

At court, I hear rumours of a pageant being prepared—a dramatic recreation, a symbolic ritual.

No one will say what part I'll play.

But when I walk past a storage room, I see a seamstress sewing a white veil edged in gold.

My throat tightens.

And I don't know if it's fear or understanding.

That night, I sit in silence. I do not hold the wooden cup. I do not whisper my name.

Instead, I write it with my finger in the condensation on the windowpane: Aeneas.

The name fades before I finish.

But I remember where the letters were.

CHAPTER 5:

THE PART I WAS GIVEN

"On the stage, we are all someone else. Only death returns us to ourselves."

— Petronius, Satyricon

Rome —65 CE

The announcement comes at the end of a private banquet, delivered in the emperor's own voice—casual and bright:

"This spring, we shall offer Rome a display worthy of its history. A reenactment of divine union—tragedy, beauty, rebirth. Art, elevated through truth."

He smiles, drinks, and the guests murmur their appreciation.

I already know it involves me.

In the days that follow, scrolls travel back and forth between palace and theatre. Costumes are designed, chariots requisitioned, musicians hired. Nothing is said to me directly, but fragments reach my ears:

"The empress's likeness is uncanny."

"Nero insists on authenticity."

"It must be tasteful. But unforgettable."

No one says my name. Not even when I'm in the room.

They speak of me as if I were a statue. An ornament. An echo.

When I finally receive the script, it arrives on cream-coloured parchment, folded in silk.

There are no lines for me to speak.

Only stage directions:

"Enter as imperial bride, crowned in lilies. Kneel. Extend the right hand. Smile."

That is all.

The man playing Nero will speak for both of us—

a condemned prisoner, chosen for his resemblance, for the sake of accuracy.

He has no name either.

At rehearsal, I stand at the centre of the amphitheatre, dressed in white robes I did not choose, while costumers tug at seams and makeup artists adjust the tint of my cheeks.

"You'll be radiant," one says, brushing powder across my temple. "He'll weep."

He.

The emperor will not perform this time. He will watch from a private box.

At least, that is what they say.

The stage manager approaches. "Try lifting your chin more. Look trusting. Innocent. Willing."

I try.

I fail.

"That's better," he lies.

Afterwards, I sit alone in the dressing chamber while an attendant unpins my hair.

He doesn't meet my eyes.

Neither do I.

Back at the palace, the corridors feel narrower than before, the walls closer. I begin to notice how few doors open from the inside.

I no longer share meals with others. My food is delivered to my room. When I eat, I forget to taste.

Alexios visits once.

He says nothing about the pageant.

He only looks at me, frowns, and leaves a small pouch on the table. Inside is a vial of oil, a comb, and a gold clasp.

Tools. Not gifts.

Tools to keep me presentable.

At night, I can no longer sleep in silence.

I hum to myself—low, tuneless, broken sounds, just to keep from falling too far inward.

Sometimes I say my name out loud. Just once. No more.

Aeneas.

It doesn't echo.

One morning, a new costume appears.

It's not white.

It's pink—soft, translucent, cinched at the waist with a woven golden belt.

A bridal tunic.

An hour passes before I touch it.

Crying is not something I do.

I haven't cried since the day they measured me for the first time, when I realised none of the men in the room said my name either.

On the final rehearsal day, they gave me a ring.

Not the first, not the last—just another adornment. A pearl set in bronze.

"Symbolic," says the woman as she places it on my finger. "The emperor wants Rome to remember what it means to be devoted."

I nod.

But I'm no longer sure if she's talking about the dead empress—or about me.

The theatre itself is a jewel box of carved stone and linen banners, refurbished for the occasion.

The seats gleam with fresh polish. The orchestra has rehearsed for weeks. Flowers line the aisles.

And in the centre: the altar.

At the signal, I will be led down a marble staircase in a veil. I will kneel beside the mock emperor. I will be crowned. And I will smile.

Because that is the part I was given.

The day arrives.

They dress me without speaking.

I wear the veil.

I walk barefoot down the service corridor while flute music floats above like smoke.

The heat from the torches presses against my cheeks. Sweat slides down my spine, unnoticed by the attendants who brush powder across my jawline and tuck strands of hair behind my ears.

I wait at the edge of the curtain, just out of sight, listening as the audience settles into their rows.

Thousands.

Noble families. Senators. Foreign dignitaries.

They will all see me.

And they will not see me.

A hush falls.

The cue is given.

The curtain lifts.

And I walk.

The robe flows behind me. The lilies in my hair itch. My feet feel far from the ground.

I move as I was taught—graceful, composed, hollow.

The crowd inhales as I appear.

I feel the instant they recognise the face I carry.

Not mine.

Hers.

The dead empress—wife of Nero, loved, mourned, mythologised.

Reborn in a boy's skin, draped in a state-funded costume.

I reach the altar.

I kneel.

The actor beside me—blond, broad-shouldered, trembling—grasps my hand and repeats the vows Nero once made in private chambers no one remembers.

I extend my hand.

I smile.

The crowd watches.

The music swells.

And for one terrifying moment, I feel myself disappear.

But I don't.

Not entirely.

Inside the veil, behind the smile, beneath the silk and stage and symmetry, I remain.

The dead empress is not me.

I am not a symbol.

I am not their display.

I am the boy from Bithynia who once sat beside an olive press and watched sunlight turn to gold.

And no one—not an emperor, not a god—can make me forget that.

When the ceremony ends, the applause rolls like thunder.

I rise. I bow. I turn.

And I walk back into the wings.

Alone in the dressing room, I remove the veil and stare at my reflection.

The powder is cracking at the edges.

The rouge is smudged.

I look almost human.

I sit beside the mirror and press my thumb into my palm, just to feel something real.

Tomorrow, they will praise me.

They will send gifts, gestures, and smiles that never reach their eyes.

They will speak of beauty, of art, of devotion.

But I will remember the silence behind the applause—

And the hand I kept clenched behind the curtain.

CHAPTER 6:

THE PROPERTY OF MEMORY

"What the gods love, they preserve. What they preserve, they destroy."

— Anonymous, Temple inscription

Rome — 66 CE

The spectacle ends. The applause fades. But I do not return to the Senator's house.

The carriage rolls toward a villa outside the city walls—larger, quieter, shrouded by cypress trees. New guards. New corridors. New silence.

This place belongs to Tigellinus, Prefect of the Praetorian Guard—Nero's enforcer, a man who collects secrets and people with equal efficiency.

He doesn't greet me personally. Instead, a servant leads me to a marble room with no furniture except a narrow bed and a bronze basin.

"You'll be summoned," the man says. "Until then, wait."

Three days pass. No one speaks to me. Food appears. Robes are changed. The lilies in the vase are replaced each morning. But no one calls me by name.

Then Tigellinus appears.

"You've made quite an impression," he says. "Nero wanted to keep you close, but emperors fall in love with illusions. They grow tired. Or guilty."

He steps closer. "But the rest of us see value where he sees distraction."

I don't answer.

"I've acquired custody. Not just for pleasure—for leverage." He lifts a lock of my hair, studies it, then lets it fall. "You are a living artefact. A reminder. A threat. A gift. Depending on who holds you."

Days blur into a new routine. Not touched, but watched. Displayed for senators, diplomats, and ambassadors who speak in careful euphemisms while I stand silent as a painted vase.

"She moves just like her," one murmurs.

"Not moves," Tigellinus replies. "Breathes."

I hear them. I hear everything.

At night, I lie still and recite the names I'm losing:

Son. Brother. Aeneas. Boy.

They once felt like anchors. Now they feel like fingerprints on glass—visible only in certain light, easily wiped away.

Within days, I overhear Tigellinus speaking with a messenger.

"He may send for her again," the man says.

"She is not his anymore," Tigellinus replies. "He gave her up the moment he put her on stage."

I'm not sure who they're talking about. I suspect they aren't sure either.

The transfer to Otho happens without ceremony. Another villa, another dangerous man with charming eyes and a different kind of hunger.

"I've seen the paintings," he says. "But they don't do you justice."

He walks around me in a slow circle. It's familiar now.

"I won't harm you," he says. "Not unless you force me to."

With Otho, the display changes again. No lilies, no veils, no ceremonies. Only private dinners where he stares, drinks, and forgets I'm not her.

He doesn't call me by the dead empress's name. He doesn't call me Aeneas either. He doesn't call me anything.

Once, after too much wine, he grips my wrist too tightly, then apologises too softly.

"I'm not like him," he says, meaning Nero.

Then he kisses my neck and says nothing for an hour.

Some nights I feel myself retreat—a small pulling back, a shrinking, like a thread slipping loose from a seam.

I learn how to look without looking. To walk without arriving. To be present in body and absent in meaning.

It isn't an escape. But it's something.

Weeks pass. Outside, Rome whispers of rebellion. Still, I remain—a living reminder of a woman who is gone, and a boy who no longer answers when called.

One morning, while Otho is away, I find a parchment on his writing desk. A list of names. Mine is not on it.

But at the bottom, "Sporus" appears: Prepare for return to Nero.

I stare at it for a long time. The name is foreign. Sharp. Small. But something tells me it's meant for me.

Sporus. Spoiled seed. Castrated one. A joke turned into a wound, a wound made into a title. A replacement for the name they've worn out.

That night, I take the name into my mouth. Just once. I taste it.

I do not swallow.

They will pass me between themselves until I break or vanish. Not because they hate me, but because I'm useful. Because I remind them of what they lost. Because I carry a shape they desire. Because power must inhabit flesh to feel real.

But they still don't know what remains inside me that I whisper names into the dark. That I press my fingertips into my palm, just to feel where the skin is still mine. That I remember the sound of oil dripping into a jar, and my father's hand steadying mine.

I was a boy. I became a shadow. Now I am a memory, passed from mouth to mouth.

But I am not erased. Not yet.

CHAPTER 7:

THE EMPEROR'S END

"Power dies with its holder, but the powerless carry their chains to the grave."

— Tacitus, Histories

Rome — Early 68 CE

They summon me again.

The guards wear Nero's crest, but their eyes are tired. Their armour is scratched. One carries a scroll; the other does not speak.

"You're to return to the palace," the first says. "The emperor requests you."

The word requests has lost meaning.

So has the emperor.

I am escorted through the city at night, past shuttered shops and quiet streets. Rome feels different now—less like a body, more like a carcass. The air is heavy, too still, as if something is holding its breath.

No crowds.

No music.

No watchers.

Only torches and silence.

The palace is quieter, too. Fewer servants. The hallways echo.

I am brought to a new chamber. Not the room I once occupied, perfumed and painted. This one is bare stone, with a narrow bed and no windows.

It smells of vinegar and ash.

They leave me there.

No one says how long.

The next morning, I am summoned to the emperor's private quarters.

Not the grand throne room. Not the hall of mirrors.

A smaller space—candlelit, curtains drawn.

Nero sits alone on a low couch, wrapped in a red cloak. His hair is dishevelled. His eyes are darker than I remember—not tired, but distant.

He does not stand when I enter.

He does not speak for a long time.

Finally, he lifts a hand.

"You're still beautiful," he says.

It is not a compliment.

It is a confession—a last act of superstition.

I say nothing.

He studies me like a man reaching for a memory just out of grasp.

"I dreamed of her again," he murmurs. "But she wouldn't speak. She only stared at me. And your face was hers."

He reaches for a goblet and drinks. Wine stains his mouth.

"I should have let you go," he says. "Long ago."

In the days that follow, I remain in the palace.

Not adorned. Not displayed.

Just kept—

a shadow in the background of a dying reign.

Outside the walls, Rome whispers.

Of plots. Armies. Betrayals.

Senators defect. Generals pledge loyalty to new emperors.

Nero holds festivals. He sings.

He drags the theatre into his own collapsing myth.

One night, I am brought to a small gathering in the imperial garden.

It is meant to be private. Intimate.

But no one speaks above a murmur, and the laughter is brittle.

Nero wears a wreath of gold leaves and recites lines from Greek tragedy. When he finishes, no one applauds.

He turns to me.

"Sporus," he says.

The name lands like a pebble in still water.

"Sporus, come sit beside me."

I obey.

He takes my hand.

"Would you die with me?" he asks.

The garden holds its breath.

"I need someone who understands."

Later, I lie awake in the dark and try to feel something.

Fear.

Pity.

Resolve.

Instead, I feel a small, quiet seed of survival take root beneath my ribs.

I will not die for Nero.

I will not be buried with his dreams.

The end comes quickly.

News reaches the palace that the Senate has declared him an enemy of the state. The Praetorians abandon him. Galba's revolt has succeeded.

Nero flees.

I am taken with him.

We hide in a villa on the outskirts: four of us— a freedman, two guards, and me.

He paces. He weeps. He shouts.

He asks if history will remember him as an artist.

He asks me if I think he was loved.

I don't answer.

He doesn't notice.

He no longer sees me.

He never did.

The sound of hoofbeats in the distance ends it.

He panics. Screams.

Orders his freedman to help him die.

I am told to leave the room.

But I hear the blade.

I hear the gasp.

I hear the silence that follows.

When I am brought back in, his face is already turning grey.

A pool of blood seeps into the floor.

His fingers twitch once, then stop.

Someone closes his eyes.

No one speaks.

The men look at me, uncertain.

The emperor is dead.

But I am still here.

They do not return me to the palace.

They do not free me.

I am handed to Nymphidius Sabinus, the new Praetorian commander.

He wants me as a symbol—

not of beauty, but of continuity.

He parades me at formal gatherings, makes me ride in his chariot, and calls me "the empress who survived."

He says it with a smile,

but I feel the steel beneath it.

Each man who holds me believes I mean something different:

To Nero, I was memory.

To Tigellinus, leverage.

To Otho, longing.

To Sabinus, legitimacy.

To none of them was I real.

CHAPTER 8:

THE LEFTOVERS OF EMPIRE

"When the feast ends, even the golden cups are thrown away."

— Juvenal, Satires

Rome — Summer, 68 CE

They say Nero killed himself with a borrowed dagger, in a borrowed villa, beneath a borrowed sky.

They say his final words were, "What an artist dies in me."

But when I left the room, he wasn't speaking. He was gasping.

I expected the world to shift, as if Rome might exhale and break the spell. But nothing shifted. The sun still rose. The guards still marched. The system adjusted—like a snake shedding its skin and sliding forward.

I was not freed. I was handed over.

Nymphidius Sabinus—commander of the Praetorian Guard, self-declared heir to Nero's legacy—welcomed me with a rehearsed smile.

"Rome will need reminders," he said. "Symbols. Continuity."

He meant me.

At festivals, he made me hold laurel branches and scatter roses over the crowd. "See?" he would announce. "Even the empress remains faithful to the empire."

The crowds cheered—not for me, but for the memory he made me carry. They weren't looking at my face. They were looking through it.

Behind closed doors, Sabinus rehearsed speeches in front of me. He spoke of the people's love, the army's favour, and the gods' approval. He looked at me and saw prophecy.

But I saw a man who mistook power for poetry.

Once, I overheard him whisper of a new spectacle—dressing me in bridal robes and parading me before the people as if I were an empress reborn.

A week later, Sabinus was dead. The crowd turned. The army turned. Vitellius arrived, and the palace shifted again.

They didn't summon me this time. They transferred me—not to a general or an heir, but to the eunuchs' quarter in the service wing of the new imperial compound.

They gave me a room with no mirrors. A robe with no dye. A name I already knew: Sporus.

In the kitchens, no one looked directly at me. Some had heard stories, some hadn't. To most, I was just another figure moving from task to task—pouring wine, arranging spices, trimming wicks.

I began to speak again. Small words. Simple ones. Not the Greek I learned for Nero. Not the verse they had fed me. Just language. Just breath.

One of the older servants—Mara, from Crete—showed me how to keep mint alive through winter.

"You pinch the top leaves," she said. "Not the sides. If you cut too deep, it won't regrow."

I nodded. I tended the mint carefully.

I began to dream again—not of Rome, but of Bithynia. Of oil presses and bees. My brother is climbing olive trees barefoot. Of my father's back, bent but solid.

Of the wooden cup. I had not seen it in years, but in the dream I still held it, still whispered my name into its curve.

Then word came: the new emperor was planning games. Lavish, brutal, designed to prove strength, to silence opposition, to entertain.

And my name—Sporus—was whispered once more. Not for tribute. Not for honour. For execution.

They said he planned to have me in a wedding dress again. To bind me in white and gold. To walk me into the arena. Not to marry this time, but to die—publicly, painfully—the final joke of a dead emperor's story.

I stood in the gardens the night I heard. The moonlight touched the mint leaves. My hands smelled of thyme.

And I knew: if I did not choose now, someone else always would.

I returned to my chamber. I cleaned my hands. I sat at the edge of the cot.

And I made the last decision I would ever make alone.

I did not leave a note. I did not carve a message. I did not shout a name.

Because I was done being named.

CHAPTER 9:

BEFORE THE CURTAIN

"The only freedom left to some is the freedom to refuse one more day."

— Stoic maxim

Rome — Autumn, 69 CE

They don't say it aloud. They never do.

But I hear it in the silence after the orders are given—in the rustle of fabric laid out on the stone bench outside my chamber, in the way the guards glance at me and then away.

I've been chosen. Again.

The games are scheduled for the end of the month. Vitellius wants to mark his reign with spectacle—blood, beauty, obedience.

And what better symbol than me? Sporus. The empress who wouldn't die. The ghost of Nero's shame, reborn in silk.

They plan to dress me as a bride again. To walk me into the arena. This time, not for vows—for the lions.

There is no rage in me. No sobbing. No shaking. Only a kind of stillness I've learned from marble statues and empty rooms.

This is not punishment. It is the inevitable conclusion of a joke that stopped being funny a long time ago.

That night, I walk alone through the inner garden. Mara is pruning the mint in silence. She nods at me. I nod back.

The moon hangs soft and low, curled like a slice of citrus in a bowl of stars. The fountains are off, waterless. Even Rome seems to know the time for spectacles is ending.

I sit by the pond, where fish once swam before they were boiled for the banquet of an emperor who lasted only ten weeks.

I dip my fingers into the cold stone basin—not to cleanse anything, but simply to feel something that hasn't been claimed.

I've worn the robes. Spoken the words. Held the smiles steady through song and wine and death.

But not one of them ever asked me what I saw. None of them ever asked who I was when the curtain dropped.

So before I go, I will say it—if only to myself.

I saw emperors cry in private. I saw slaves refuse to flinch. I saw love turned into a ceremony and grief carved into laws. I watched men burn cities to keep their names on lips for one more season.

And I learned that power feeds on what it takes from others.

In Nero, I saw a boy who wanted to be eternal. And in myself, I saw someone he thought would hold his reflection.

But I wasn't a mirror. I was a vessel. And he poured poison into it, called it wine, and waited for applause.

Let them remember me as Sporus, if they must. Let the name echo through marble halls and brittle scrolls.

But the truth is simpler. I am not Sporus. I am not the dead empress. I am not anyone's second draft.

I was a boy from Bithynia. I had a brother who made me laugh by balancing figs on his head—three at once, wobbling like a crown. Even in memory, it makes me smile.

I had a wooden cup, small and cracked, stained with olive oil and love, and a father who spoke my name like a prayer he never needed answered.

That is who I am. That is who I take with me.

I do not fear death. What I fear is one more day in which someone else writes the caption beneath my image, one more morning when I wake and must wear the shape of another's sorrow, one more breath spent waiting for a cue.

I light a lamp. I wash my hands. I press my fingers to the wall where someone long ago carved a crude name.

It is faded, illegible. But I like to think it mattered to someone once.

I whisper: Aeneas. Not a myth. Not a hero. Just a boy.

Then I lie back, holding the blade close to my chest, like the wooden cup I once carried.

The edge is sharp, but not cruel.

I am not afraid.

Because for the first time in years, I get to end the scene.

EPILOGUE

In my final silence, I was not empty.
I did not vanish.
I was not erased.
They named me after a joke.
They dressed me like a ghost.
They kissed me like a grave.
But that was their story.
Mine is quieter.
I was born by an olive grove.
I knew the scent of pressed fruit and sun-warmed dust.
I held a wooden cup, carved by my father's hand.
It cracked in the fire.
But even broken, it could still hold light.
I loved once, though no one ever asked whom.
I laughed, though they never wrote that down.
I wept in silence when silence was the only safety left.
I learned the art of vanishing without disappearing.
They passed me hand to hand like a relic.
But I am not a relic.

I am the root.

I am origin.

I am the breath that left the stage before the curtain fell.

And if someday, in a quiet archive or a brittle scroll, someone reads my name—

Or the name they gave me—

Let them wonder.

Let them feel the hollow where I once stood.

Let them ask:

Who was he, really?

Let that question echo longer than any answer Rome dared to give.

Because I was never just what they saw.

I was Aeneas.

And I lived.

HIEROCLES

The Emperor's Consort, the Charioteer's Crown

PROLOGUE

They think they know my story.

The mad emperor who dressed as a woman. The beautiful charioteer who seduced him. The scandal that proved Rome was falling into Eastern decadence.

Simple. Clean. Wrong.

I lived through what they've turned into myth. I was there when the boy-priest from Syria tried to remake an empire's soul, when sacred and profane blurred until you couldn't tell transformation from destruction. I felt her hands reshape my body, heard her voice rename my purpose, watched her love consume everything it touched—including herself.

The historians write about excess and corruption. They reduce us to cautionary tales about power gone mad. But they weren't in the palace when the incense burned and the boundaries dissolved. They didn't see what I saw, feel what I felt, choose what I chose.

They call her reign a footnote. An aberration was quickly corrected.

I call it the time I learned that survival sometimes looks like surrender, that beauty can be both weapon and wound, and that the most radical thing you can do in a world that wants to transform you is to choose your own ending.

This is what really happened in those gilded rooms.

This is how I lived through it.

CHAPTER 1:

THE TRACK

"In the reign of Elagabalus, all the traditions of Rome were overturned, and the sacred mixed with the profane in ways that offended both gods and men."

— Cassius Dio, Roman History

Rome, 218 CE

The sand never leaves you. It gets under your nails, between your teeth, works its way into cuts until you're part of the track, whether you like it or not. I've been breathing Circus dust for six years now and still wake up spitting grit.

The noise? That's not cheering—it's hunger. Sixty thousand throats wanting blood, wanting to see something break. They don't care if it's a wheel or a neck, as long as it's loud when it snaps.

I learned that lesson early.

I'm not the fastest driver in Rome. Not even close. But I know what the crowd wants, and I know how to give it to them without dying. That's worth more than speed. The Greens pay me to look good losing, and I'm damn good at it.

"Beautiful disaster," they call me. Golden hair that catches the light just right, a scar across my shoulder where a wheel hub kissed me two summers back. Enough to make the ladies sigh and the men bet stupid money. The crowd loves a pretty boy who might not make it to the finish line.

The other factions noticed, of course.

The Reds tried to buy me out. The Blues offered double what the Greens were paying. The Whites just threw rocks—but even their hate was useful. Hate sells tickets same as love.

See, the Circus isn't a sport. It's politics in harnes. Blue wins, the grain ships run on time. Green takes a race, a good harvest is coming. Red crashes, somebody's going to war. White does anything, and the gods are pissed about something.

We're not drivers. We're omens on legs.

The other charioteers figured that out too late. They kept treating it like a competition—about honour and fair play, may the most deserving man win. Meanwhile, I was watching the imperial box, counting who was betting what, measuring which way the wind was blowing.

That's the way I saw her looking.

Not the usual watchers—senators' wives slumming for thrills, merchants hunting for opportunities. This was different. Patient. Calculating. Like she was measuring me for something specific.

The gifts started small: leather oil for my reins, a better grade than I could afford; wine that tasted like it cost more than my monthly earnings; a note wrapped around a wheel spoke: For one who understands the pageant.

Display. The right word for it.

The other drivers got pissy about the attention. They started the usual tricks—loosened buckles, stones in feed bags, oil on the track before my turns. Amateur hour stuff. If you're going to sabotage someone, do it right.

They never figured out that the real game wasn't about winning races.

The day everything changed, I wasn't even trying to finish.

My lead bay went down hard in the final turn. Not an accident—I saw the rock fly from the stands, watched it arc like it had eyes. A perfect throw, right into his front legs. Professional work.

I had maybe two heartbeats to decide: try to save the horse and wreck myself, or cut left and save the chariot.

I cut left. Hard.

The wheel came off the ground, the whole rig balanced on nothing but momentum and prayer. I brought it down clean, but the race was done. The Blues thundered past while I limped my team off the sand.

That's when I saw her.

Waiting in the tunnel like smoke with a face.

Emperor Elagabalus. The priest-king who'd been scandalising Rome since she was fourteen. Silk robes that shifted colour when she moved, eyes lined thick with kohl, lips dark as dried blood. When she came close, I smelled frankincense and roses—and something underneath that made my skin crawl.

"You drive like you're running toward something," she said.

I didn't bow. Didn't see the point.

"Most people run from death," she continued. "You run toward transformation."

"I run toward the finish line."

She smiled. Not pleasantly. "Same thing, in the end."

She turned to go, then stopped. "You dream of falling."

It wasn't a question. I'd never told anyone about those dreams.

"Falling's just flying without style," I said.

Her laugh was as sharp as broken glass. "Perfect."

Then she was gone, leaving nothing but perfume and the sense that I had just signed a bond I hadn't read.

After that, the real gifts began to arrive.

First: a racing chariot worth more than most houses—green and gold, built for show rather than speed. Four white horses came with it, imported from somewhere east of everything, each worth a senator's yearly income.

I raced it once. Not to win, but to be seen. The crowd fell silent when I appeared, as if they were witnessing something sacred. Maybe they were.

When I climbed down after that final spectacle, her guards were waiting.

"You're called," one said.

I didn't ask where. I already knew my racing days were over.

What I didn't know was that what came next would be worse.

CHAPTER 2:

THE GILDED CAGE

"The palace consumed all who entered it, but some it transformed into gold before the devouring."

— Augustan History

Rome, 219 CE

First thing about the Palatine: it's designed to make you feel small.

Every doorway is too tall, every corridor too wide, every statue staring down like it knows something you don't. Standard intimidation tactics. I'd seen the same setup at the bigger racing stables—make the new boys feel grateful just to be there.

The difference was, this place had the budget to do it right.

The guards didn't even blink when I walked through. I was covered in dust, blood under my nails, smelling of horse sweat and honest work. I should've been thrown out on sight. Instead, they bowed.

Not to me—to whatever orders brought me here.

That told me everything about how deep I was already in.

The procession through the palace was pure theatre. Rose petals scattered ahead of my feet—wasteful but effective. Eunuchs posed in doorways like living decorations. Even the servants moved like dancers, every motion choreographed to impress the rubes.

I kept my face blank. Rule one of performing: never let them see you're impressed, even when you are.

But the marble got to me anyway. Columns that belonged in temples, not houses. Mosaics that cost more than entire neighbourhoods. And everywhere, the smell—not the honest stench of stables, but something artificial. Perfume, power, and the particular scent of people who'd forgotten what real work felt like.

Three courtyards, two waiting rooms, one door that probably cost more than my entire neighbourhood. When it opened, the voice that came out was honey over steel.

"Enter."

The room inside was a stage set. Silk drapes shifting to rhythms I couldn't track. Musicians playing instruments I'd never seen, sounds that made your skin crawl in interesting ways. Incense thick enough to chew—Syrian frankincense mixed with something that tasted like distant temples.

And centre stage: Elagabalus.

She was draped across a couch like she was posing for a statue. Her robe was sewn with pearls that chimed when she breathed. Her hair was piled into a tower that must've taken hours to build, adorned with Syrian diadems. Her eyes were lined so thick with kohl they looked like holes cut in porcelain.

Beautiful. Terrifying. Completely artificial.

Perfect predator.

"You're filthier than I hoped," she said, then smiled as though she'd just unwrapped a present. "Wonderful."

She waved a hand. Musicians, servants, painted boys—everyone vanished like smoke. When we were alone, she stood and walked toward me. Barefoot. Silent. A predator approaching prey.

She circled me once, then twice, breathing in my scent as though she were tasting wine.

"These hands will have to change," she said, lifting my fingers to examine the calluses. Each ridge and rough patch was mapped by fingertips that had never known honest work. "But the eyes… yes. They still remember the sky."

"What do you see when you look at me?" I asked.

Her smile was sharp as broken glass. "Potential."

The makeover started that same hour.

Not all at once—too obvious. Instead, it unfolded like a campaign. Each day, something new disappeared. Each night, something else was reshaped.

First came the body hair. They led me to a chamber that stank of sulphur and burned herbs, where three slaves waited with bowls of paste that looked like mud from the underworld.

"This will hurt," one said, not unkindly.

It did. The paste felt like liquid fire eating through my skin, leaving me raw and smooth as a temple statue. I bit my tongue bloody to keep from screaming. When they finally scraped it off with bronze blades, I didn't recognise the skin beneath.

"Better," said the lead slave, stepping back to admire his work. "Now you look like someone worth transforming."

The baths came next. Not washing—ritual. Hours soaking in oils that smelled like places I'd never been. Servants scrubbed until I glowed like polished marble. Different perfumes for different parts of my body—roses for my chest, sandalwood for my arms, something that smelled like distant rain for my hair.

"You're being prepared for presentation," one of the bath attendants explained as he worked scented oil into my shoulders. "The empress wants you perfect."

"Perfect for what?"

He didn't answer. But his hands paused in their work, and I saw something—pity, perhaps—flash across his face.

Then came the voice lessons.

Marcus Aurelius—not the philosopher, but a eunuch from Alexandria who'd been castrated young enough to keep his musical voice. He had intelligent eyes and hands that moved like birds when he spoke.

"You sound like a charioteer," he said during our first session, not unkindly. "All shouts and commands. We need to make you into music."

"What's wrong with how I sound?"

"Nothing—if you want to spend your life talking to horses." He gestured for me to sit on a cushioned stool. "But if you want to survive in this place, you need to learn that words are weapons. Sharp ones cut. Musical ones seduce."

The lessons were torture of a different kind: hours spent repeating syllables until my throat ached, learning to pause where I wanted to rush, to suggest where I wanted to demand. My natural voice—the one that had shouted encouragement to horses and curses at broken wheels—was buried deeper each day.

"Better," Marcus said after two weeks of this. "You're starting to sound like someone who deserves to be listened to."

But when I heard myself speak now, I listened to a stranger wearing my throat.

They gave me quarters in the eastern wing during this transformation—three rooms bigger than any place I'd ever lived. Ceilings painted like sky—but not honest sky, the kind you saw over racing tracks. This was sky as the gods might see it: all golden light and perfect clouds that never brought rain.

The furniture was a museum of wealth—couches that cost more than horses, tables carved from single pieces of wood that had been growing before Rome was founded. Even the chamber pot was made of porcelain that sang when you tapped it.

My clothes hung in a cedar wardrobe like religious vestments. Tunics in colours that had special names—not blue, but "midnight over water"; not red, but "blood of sacrificed doves." Each piece of fabric is worth more than most people earn in a year.

I tried them on once, just to see. The silk felt like wearing air, but air that suffocated. When I moved, the fabric whispered secrets I didn't want to know.

The servants who attended me were polite professionals, doing their jobs with the efficiency of people who understood their survival depended on invisibility. They dressed me, fed me, cleaned my rooms—all while treating me like expensive furniture that needed regular maintenance.

But it was the eunuchs who showed something like warmth. They brushed my hair with the gentle attention of people preparing something sacred, oiled my shoulders as though anointing a sacrifice. One of them—barely older than me, with eyes that held too much knowledge—whispered while he worked:

"They break you slow here. Not chains. Honey."

When I asked what he meant, he only smiled and continued braiding my hair with practised fingers.

"Did you choose this?" I asked.

His hands paused. "Choice is a luxury few of us can afford."

"Do you regret it?"

He considered this while working oil into my shoulders, transforming skin that had once known sun and wind into something suited for shadowed rooms.

"I regret forgetting what I used to want," he said at last.

The next morning, I found a fig wrapped in silk on my pillow. It tasted like somewhere real, somewhere people still chose their own names.

But confiscation crushed me.

Three weeks into my transformation, I woke to find my racing tunic gone—the one piece of my old life I had smuggled in, hidden at the bottom of a chest like contraband.

In its place lay a note written in elegant script: The past is a poor fit for your future.

Beside it was a new tunic, silk so fine it felt like wearing air, dyed in a colour with no name in any language I knew.

That was the moment I realised the palace wasn't changing me—it was erasing me.

I sat on the edge of my golden bed, holding silk that cost more than everything I had ever owned, and understood that the boy who once drove chariots in the Circus was disappearing. Not killed—that would have been kinder. Just... erased of existence, replaced with something more suitable for imperial purposes.

The first time Elagabalus touched me was in her private garden, after a ceremony that left the air thick with smoke and whispered prayers. The space was smaller than I expected, more intimate: olive trees shaped into spirals, a fountain where bronze dolphins poured water into basins carved from stones I could not name.

She moved as though she owned not just the garden but the air itself. When she placed her hand on my chest, fingers tracing bones that still showed beneath the softness they were building, I felt my heartbeat shift.

"This is what Rome fears most," she said, her voice barely above a whisper.

"What?"

"You. Not man, not woman. Not a slave, not a citizen. You don't fit their boxes." Her fingers traced the line of my collarbone. "That's power they can't control."

I heard envy in her voice. Or perhaps recognition.

She looked at me as if I were a mirror—or maybe a rough draft she intended to improve.

"What happens when the transformation is complete?" I asked.

Her smile was sharp enough to cut. "Then you become everything you were always meant to be."

"And what's that?"

"Mine."

Some days, I wanted to scream. To scrape the paint off my face, tear the silk from my body, and run back to honest sweat and bruises, I could understand. To find a horse that didn't care what I looked like and ride until we both remembered what freedom felt like.

But every time rebellion rose in my chest, I remembered: guards at every gate, silence in every corridor swallowing questions before they could be asked, and her presence always there—watching from across rooms, from garden shadows, from the space between waking and sleeping where the real changes happened.

She didn't speak of love.

She spoke of destiny.

The same thing, in her world.

Sometimes you survive by letting others remake you completely, then hoping you can still gather pieces of yourself afterwards.

If anything remains.

If there is still a self-worth finding.

CHAPTER 3:

THE GAMES THEY PLAY

"In the court of Elagabalus, truth was the only coin without value."

— Lost fragment, Herodian

Rome, 219 CE

Nobody tells the truth at the palace. Ever.

At the Circus, lies got you killed. A horse either runs fast or it doesn't. A wheel either holds or it breaks. Simple.

Here, truth comes wrapped in compliments, buried under poetry nobody understands. Everyone arrives with flowers and leaves carrying your secrets.

The first invitation came from Senator Drusus—a politician with dead eyes and a handshake like a business deal. The note arrived in a bronze bird's beak:

"You are welcome among those who matter. Sunset. Hall of Victories."

I wore simple clothes: a blue tunic, minimal jewellery. I thought I was being modest.

Really, I was proclaimingthat I didn't know the rules yet.

The hall blazed with ambition disguised as a dinner party. Courtiers arranged themselves by rank, every seat placement a message. The food was built like architecture—towers of peacock, pyramids of dates, bread carved to look like the emperor's face.

They seated me next to a Vestal Virgin whose silence cut deeper than insults, across from a poet who offered wine mixed with something that made colours brighter and lies easier to swallow.

I declined. He smiled like I had just confirmed a bet.

The testing started during the fish course.

Drusus tapped his cup and started talking about horses, casually.

"I've always admired the Green teams," he said, his voice carrying across the suddenly quiet room. "So passionate. Risk everything for glory."

Every eye turned my way—the only Green in the room.

A Spanish senator replied, smooth as oil: "Passion without discipline is chaos. The Blues are strategic. Controlled. Built to last."

Murmurs of agreement. Smiles at my silence.

Classic setup: see if I'd defend my old team or bow to my new position.

"What do you think, Hierocles?" Drusus asked. "Do the Greens still hold your heart?"

The room held its breath.

I lifted my cup. "A heart's like a racing team—it changes drivers depending on who owns the track."

Laughter. Relief. Approval.

I'd passed their first test. But now I understood what kind of race this was, not around a track, but through a maze where the walls shifted and the finish line kept moving.

Afterwards, I watched a noblewoman challenge a general to a dice game. The stakes seemed simple—his horse against her jewellery. She lost on purpose. Two weeks later, I discovered the truth. His horse was worthless, fit for nothing but breeding. Her "jewellery" was a seal ring granting access to imperial mail. She'd traded a lame horse for his secrets.

Nothing was what it seemed. Everything had three meanings, two of them lies.

Elagabalus rarely appeared at these smaller gatherings, but her shadow was always present—nervous glances at empty chairs, conversations breaking off at the sound of her name.

Sometimes I glimpsed her on balconies or behind screens. She'd catch my eye across a crowded room, smile, then vanish. It made me wonder if I was imagining it.

The courtiers noticed. In a world where glances meant elevation or exile, every look was catalogued.

They began testing me differently—not just for loyalty, but for favour.

"You've grown pale," someone would remark. "Divine light bleaching you, or just the absence of sun?"

Or: "Such regal silence. One forgets you weren't born to discretion."

Always smiling, always waiting for the reaction that might reveal my true standing.

I learned to answer in riddles: Change comes in many forms. The ear learns new songs when the heart stops listening to old ones.

Survival meant becoming unreadable.

In the pre-dawn hours, I walked the gardens alone—the only time the walls didn't press inward.

One morning, a young soldier waited by the lion fountain. Bronze eyes, sword sheathed, standing where the palace windows couldn't see him.

"You're the charioteer," he said.

I nodded.

"She'll destroy you." Matter-of-fact. No emotion.

"There was another before you," he continued. "Good kid. Gentle. The court ate him alive."

"What happened?"

"Tried to leave."

"Did he succeed?"

His smile was winter-sharp. "Nobody leaves her. They just change form."

He walked away before I could ask more. But later that day, I saw him again—posted at her door, standing at attention, eyes fixed on some point beyond the horizon.

His warning echoed in my ribs.

I began collecting allies, carefully.

A dancer from Antioch taught me gesture language. A former scribe whispered which names to avoid. A priestess marked dangerous days on my calendar in saffron ink.

And then there was Zoticus.

Tall, controlled, beautiful like marble given breath. He didn't treat me as a rival or a pet but as something more complex—a successor, perhaps. Or a warning made flesh.

"I was where you are," he told me once. "Different role, though."

"What role?"

He looked at me with something that might have been pity. "One that ends quietly."

It was a new kind of race, not in the arena but through a maze where the walls were whispers and the only prize was survival.

Learning the rules.

CHAPTER 4:

THE UNMAKING

"To be loved by a god is to be unmade and remade in their image."

— Temple inscription, Emesa

Rome, 220 CE

I lost my edge first.

Not all at once, but worn away like stone under water—each day a little duller, each response a little less certain. I began hesitating before I spoke, unsure what might come out.

At night, I dreamed of shouting warnings to horses that couldn't hear me. I woke with my throat raw and my mouth full of nothing.

They kept records now. Everything was tracked.

What I ate. When I slept, how long did I spend in the baths? Servants weighed me weekly and adjusted oils accordingly. Face paints were mixed fresh each morning to match my changing skin—paler where the sun no longer touched, golden where their treatments worked their magic.

No more going outside alone. Even garden walks were timed, supervised, and reported. If I sought a brief solitude, a eunuch was always there among the greenery, feigning an inspection of the plants while watching me with contrite eyes.

Not gaolers. Curators.

The voice master returned with new exercises: Syrian love songs, scraps of Sappho, dialogues between gods and mortals where boundaries blurred and disappeared. He made me whisper them, sing them, breathe them like prayers.

"Your body might betray you," he said, fingers on my throat as he felt the vibrations. "But your voice will reveal you. It must be perfect, or it will be your ruin."

I started forgetting how I used to sound. The memory of my own voice became like a dream on waking—vivid for a moment, then gone.

The mirror in my chambers turned into an enemy.

Each morning, it showed me someone I almost recognised. Painted lips. Smooth cheeks. A softness that belonged to someone else entirely.

I looked good. Too good, in ways that made my skin crawl. One morning, I put my fist through the mirror. It cracked down the middle, splitting my face in two.

They replaced it that afternoon with polished silver, harder to break.

The next day, I couldn't remember why I'd wanted to destroy it.

I asked Elagabalus why she had chosen me.

We lay in her private chamber, skin slick with oils that smelled of frankincense and distant places. Her fingers traced my hip, my ribs, the places where muscle was slowly softening.

"Why me?" I whispered.

She studied my face as if reading auguries in bone and flesh.

"Because you understand spectacle," she said at last. "You always have. Racing was ritual—sacrifice and spectacle, movement with meaning. This—" she touched my chest, "is the same thing. Just a different costume."

"But the others before—"

"They pretended to be what I needed. You become it."

Her words settled in my bones like poison. Or prophecy.

One night, I found the young eunuch who had brought me that fig during my first week. He was weeping in a forgotten corridor, his back marked with welts, his tunic torn at the shoulder.

I knelt beside him. He flinched from my touch.

"Who did this?"

He shook his head, tears cutting tracks through the powder on his face.

Three days later, I saw him again—painted in gold and blue, rings on every finger, walking three careful steps behind some visiting prince from Mauretania.

He no longer wept. He no longer looked at me.

I understood then that kindness was a luxury neither of us could afford.

The lunar rite to Elagabal came next. Days of preparation. They painted my hands with henna spirals and dyed my feet red with crushed madder. A priestess sewed golden bells into my sleeves so I would chime like temple wind when I moved.

They gave me a name for the night: Salma, daughter of flame.

I danced.

Not entertainment—invocation. I moved as they had taught me. Slow at first, arms rising like smoke from a sacrifice. Then faster, wilder, knees bent, hair loose, sweat flying from my throat in arcs that caught the torchlight and scattered like stars.

I forgot everything—my old name, my old body, the person I had been before marble and silk transformed me. I became pure movement, pure purpose, prayer made flesh.

When the music stopped, I collapsed at Elagabalus's feet.

She did not lift me.

She only whispered: "Now you understand."

Afterwards, I was sick for days. Henna stained my skin until it peeled away in strips. The bells left bruises on my wrists like fingerprints from invisible hands. I couldn't eat without retching, couldn't sleep without dreaming of fire and falling.

I stopped asking to visit the stables. Stopped writing letters I'd never send anyway. Stopped remembering the names of other charioteers—their faces blurred like paintings left out in the rain.

Sometimes I dreamed I was back in the Circus, reins in my hands, the crowd roaring my name. But in the dream, I could never find the horses. Or the track dissolved beneath my wheels. Or the crowd chanted words I didn't recognise, in voices that weren't mine.

And yet—

There were moments, brief as lightning and precious as diamonds, when I looked at myself in water instead of mirrors, in candlelight instead of harsh sun, and thought:

This isn't destruction. This is becoming something new.

Something worthy of gods and emperors, and the kind of love that burns cities.

I told myself this story over and over—

Until the telling became the only part of me I still recognised.

Until the story felt more real than the one who first spoke it.

Until I couldn't remember which was truth and which was the beautiful lie I had learned to live inside.

But somewhere, deep down, the charioteer was still there—watching, calculating, biding his time to make his move.

CHAPTER 5:

THE COURT

"Power in the palace flowed like water—finding every crack, filling every void, shaping everything it touched."

— Anonymous court chronicle

Rome, 220 CE

Months passed like this. The changes came so gradually I stopped noticing them—until one day I caught my reflection and didn't recognise the person looking back. By the time they began inviting me to court functions, I had learned to move like someone else entirely. Palace power was more intricate than Circus politics. Every conversation was a ceremony.

At the centre was Elagabalus. Not just an emperor, but a high priest, a living god, a flame around which everything else orbited. Syrian priests from Emesa, Roman senators pretending they still mattered, and Eastern princes trading spices for proximity to power—all revolved in her orbit.

Then there were those of us with no official rank but something more valuable: access.

We were dangerous because we were wild cards. We had no senatorial dignity to preserve, no family fortunes to protect. We had only her attention—and that alone made us threats to everyone who believed power should follow traditional channels.

Zoticus navigated these currents like a master charioteer reading track conditions. Always gracious, never eager. His voice never rose above a murmur, and his laughter never lingered too long.

"Be remarkable only when required," he counselled me. "Never twice in succession."

I once watched him refuse a gift from a praetor—a jewelled bracelet worth a year's wages—with such elegant regret that the man felt honoured by the rejection.

The Praetorian Guard had its own ecosystem. The Germans were straightforward: tall, silent, loyal to whoever had most recently paid them. The Syrians served from religious conviction. The Romans were the most dangerous—older soldiers who remembered different emperors, men who had survived enough regime changes to know that everything was temporary except their own survival.

One of them, Cassianus, watched me with particular interest. He had fought in Gaul, lost his son to fever, and carried the cynical wisdom of a man who had outlived too many masters.

"You believe she's really divine?" he asked me once, quietly.

I answered carefully: "I believe she believes it."

He laughed—too loud, too long. "The most honest thing anyone has said in this place for months."

After that, they never bowed when I passed. A small rebellion—but small rebellions had a way of becoming large ones.

The eunuchs knew everything and said nothing. They were the palace's nervous system, carrying messages, preparing rituals, and hearing confessions without offering absolution. I trusted them more than senators, though less than marble statues.

Elagabalus distributed favour like a gambler throwing dice—sudden, dramatic, often destructive. She might give a courtier a cloak worth a villa, then demand it back two weeks later as an offering to the gods. Those who received the most lived in constant terror of losing it.

Once, she gave me a dagger—gold-hilted, with a serpent's head for a pommel.

"Not for protection," she said, eyes bright with amusement. "For augury."

I never used it, but kept it under my pillow. Some gifts were fewer than prophecies.

I had no official title, but the court began calling me *Adamas*, an uncut gem. Precious but rough. Valuable but dangerous. Still capable of cutting those who handled me carelessly.

Often, I was sent to entertain visitors too minor for imperial attention: Parthian merchants, African princes, philosophers from Athens who quoted Plato while studying the palace's exotic arrangements. Each audience was a ceremony. I learned to be charming without being informative, warm without being intimate, memorable without being quotable.

Every conversation was reported. I discovered this when Elagabalus repeated a joke I'd made privately, three days later, to the entire court. She laughed as if hearing it for the first time, but her eyes stayed on mine, measuring my reaction to the betrayal.

Nothing was private. Everything was intelligence.

I found sanctuary in a forgotten corridor near the old library—a passage half-blocked by scaffolding, too narrow for important people. I went there when I needed to think without being observed.

Zoticus found me there once. He sat beside me without asking permission.

"You should stop being honest," he said.

"I'm not honest anymore."

He raised an eyebrow. "That's the problem. You don't realise when you are."

We sat in comfortable silence, watching dust float in a shaft of light.

"They'll test you soon," he said before leaving.

"Who will?"

"Everyone."

Boredom was the real threat, not hatred.

To be useful was to be safe. To be entertaining was to be divine. But the moment you ceased to surprise, you ceased to matter.

I watched it happen to others: the singer whose voice cracked from too much myrrh, the dancer who repeated a gesture once too often, the young philosopher whose wit couldn't keep pace with his beauty's decline.

They didn't die. They faded—drifting to the edges of rooms, the backs of processions, forgotten corners where irrelevant people waited to be dismissed entirely.

I feared that more than assassination.

So I stayed sharp. I learned new languages, new songs, and new ways of moving that suggested different meanings. I made myself a collection of selves—offering only one at a time, keeping others in reserve.

Elagabalus called it brilliance.

I called it survival.

Same thing, in her world.

CHAPTER 6:

THE RITUAL

"The gods of Syria came to Rome not as conquerors but as seducers, offering ecstasy in place of duty."

— Ammianus Marcellinus

Rome, 220 CE

I'd seen rituals before. The Circus had its own liturgy—drums announcing the procession, faction leaders painted like war gods, entrails read in sand before races began. Even crashes were offerings.

But nothing prepared me for the rites of Elagabal.

In the inner sanctum, Elagabalus wasn't the emperor. She was an incarnation.

The black stone of Emesa—older than Rome, older than memory—rode on her shoulders during public ceremonies. At festivals, she walked backwards before its chariot, eyes closed, chanting in languages that predated Latin.

People watched in fascinated terror. Senators bowed while calculating rebellion. Women threw flowers. Children wept without knowing why.

I watched too. But not from the crowd—from the dais, wearing silk and authority I hadn't earned.

At first, I was excluded from the inner mysteries. Only full initiates could enter the high chamber where the most sacred rites were performed. I heard whispers: blood spilt there, naked bodies anointed with wine, the movements of stars read in bowls of oil that reflected impossible visions.

Zoticus emerged from one ceremony pale and shaking. When I asked what he'd witnessed, he could only whisper: "The sun... it moved. Against nature. But it happened."

His certainty was more disturbing than any tale of blood sacrifice.

Eventually, I was summoned to participate.

Two priests came at dawn—Syrian eunuchs whose eyes held the peculiar intensity of those who had seen gods face to face. They dressed me in white and blue, colours of air and fire. They anointed my forehead with oils of cedar and clove, braided my hair with gold thread, and attached tiny bells to my ankles.

"Speak only when spoken to," one instructed. "In the god's presence, silence is the highest wisdom."

My throat was already dry.

The inner sanctum was round, domed, lit by calculated shafts of sunlight falling through a perforated ceiling like golden spears. At its centre, the pool of black oil reflected nothing, as if it opened onto a void rather than depth.

Elagabalus stood at its edge, barefoot, wrapped in a robe that shifted colour with each movement. A crystal knife in one hand, a silver censer in the other.

She began to sing.

The words had no meaning I could grasp, but sound itself was meaning—cutting through air and flesh and bone, resonating in my chest until the floor vibrated beneath my feet. The oil rippled, though no wind stirred the chamber.

Then she spoke my name. Not Hierocles—the secret name she had given me.

What happened next lives outside memory.

Remember fire without heat touching my skin. Remember falling to my knees not from reverence, but because my legs no longer obeyed commands from a mind that had suddenly become very small.

When awareness returned, my lips were stained red. So were my hands.

They described it as wine laced with sacred herbs. I chose to believe them.

After that ceremony, I was marked in ways I couldn't name. People stepped aside when I approached. Courtiers bowed lower. Servants crossed themselves when they thought I wasn't watching.

Elagabalus called me her "shadow-keeper"—one who stands beside flame without being consumed.

It didn't feel holy. It felt hollowed out, as though something essential had been removed and replaced with echoes.

More rituals followed as the seasons turned: moon rites and fire rites, ceremonies of salt and milk, invocations spoken in tongues that tasted like copper and starlight.

With each ritual, I lost something—a memory, a word, a scar that had once connected me to a former life. But I gained something too: the ability to move through the palace like a force of nature rather than a person. When I entered rooms, conversations shifted. When I spoke, even senators listened.

Fear and reverence are close cousins.

But I didn't believe—not the way they wanted me to.

I believed in theatre. In the power of masks and movement to create meaning from emptiness. Rituals were real, not because gods answered them, but because people needed them to be real.

The gods might not be watching, but people certainly were. And in their eyes, I was becoming something sacred.

Which was, perhaps, the only kind of divinity that mattered.

There was one ritual I refused.

The cutting ceremony—symbolic piercing, bloodletting that would mark my flesh as belonging permanently to the god.

When they brought the golden instruments, I looked directly at Elagabalus and said, "No."

The silence that followed was absolute. Priests froze mid-gesture. Even the oil in the sacred pool seemed to be still.

She stared at me for a long moment, then turned and walked away without a word.

For three days, I existed in exile within the palace. No meals arrived. No one spoke my name.

On the fourth day, she summoned me to her private garden.

I knelt, expecting punishment or dismissal.

Instead, she cupped my face in her hands.

"You're not mine if you break," she whispered. "You're mine because you bend without breaking."

The cutting was never mentioned again.

But I understood I had passed a test I hadn't known I was taking.

Like everything else in this place—a game within a game, a ceremony within a ceremony.

The question was: how many layers deep before you hit something real?

CHAPTER 7:

ZOTICUS

"In the palace, yesterday's favourite becomes tomorrow's cautionary tale."

— Palace graffiti, found carved beneath a marble bench

Rome, 221 CE

Zoticus had been what I was becoming—beautiful, favoured, dangerous, the way a blade is dangerous to whoever holds it. But where I burned bright and unsteady, he had learned to glow with the cool light of polished marble. He was what happened when someone survived long enough to master the rules.

His beauty was built to perfection—the kind sculptors copied and poets wept over. Sharp cheekbones, pale eyes, skin that had never known real work or honest sun.

Mine was still wild, unrefined, capable of surprising even me. His was perfect, controlled, and calculated as carefully as a military campaign. His beauty served him now. Mine still served her.

We spoke more often as winter turned to spring, though never in public and never for long. Brief encounters in forgotten alcoves, conversations that began with politics and ended with confessions neither of us had planned to make.

He taught me which foods to avoid (anything that arrived without explanation), which courtiers to distrust (the ones who smiled too readily), and where never to stand when Elagabalus was in her darker moods (directly in her line of sight, but close enough to touch).

He never suggested I should leave. He knew I wouldn't.

But sometimes, in the spaces between his words, I heard regret.

"You love her?" I asked once.

We were in the tepidarium, steam rising around us like spirits of the dead. No one else had dared enter while we were there—not from any rule, but from instinctive knowledge that some conversations required absolute privacy.

Zoticus was quiet for so long, I thought he wouldn't answer.

"I loved what she made me forget," he said at last.

"What was that?"

"Myself."

He slipped beneath the water. When he surfaced, hair slicked back like a seal's, he added, "But now I remember again. That's the real danger."

Rumours followed him like smoke—planning to leave the palace, dismissed in private, his influence waning as mine grew. One senator joked at dinner that "flowers bloom beautifully, but even perfect roses eventually wilt."

Yet Zoticus remained, not as consort, not as priest, but as something more complex—a living reminder of the palace's power to transform, and perhaps a warning of its power to discard.

He told me about his predecessor—a boy I had never heard mentioned.

"A musician from Gaul," he said. "Not as beautiful as us, but full of grace. Full of genuine faith in what we were doing here."

"What happened?"

Zoticus's smile was sharp as a blade. "She made him choose."

"Between what?"

"Between the god and his body. Between serving the divine and remaining human."

"What did he choose?"

"Wrongly."

I didn't ask for details. Some knowledge was too dangerous to possess.

One night, Elagabalus made me dance for her private entertainment. Not in the temple, not for the court—just for her, in a chamber filled with cushions and burning amber.

She lay on silk cushions, wine-flushed, clapping as I moved through the steps I had learned in sacred rites. When I spun, my robes flared like wings. When I bent, the bells on my ankles sang like trapped birds.

"You're better than he was," she murmured, eyes bright with wine and memory.

I didn't need to ask who she meant.

But I wondered if Zoticus had danced for her like this, in this same room, wearing these same bells. If she had told him he was better than whoever came before. If she already imagined someone better than me.

The last time I saw Zoticus, he was standing in the hall of imperial portraits—a gallery of marble faces representing five centuries of Roman power.

He stood before the newest addition: Elagabalus rendered in idealised stone, her features softened into classical perfection, the most controversial aspects of her reign transformed into timeless beauty.

"Think she'll be remembered?" I asked.

He didn't turn. "She'll become a myth. Which is worse than being forgotten."

"Why?"

"Myths consume the people they're based on. She'll become a story about a lunatic emperor who dressed as a woman, married men, and violated every sacred tradition. The truth—that she was trying to transform the empire—will disappear."

"And us?"

Now he looked at me, and I saw something I'd never seen before in his perfect features: pity.

"If we're lucky, we'll disappear before they start telling stories."

The next morning, his chambers were empty.

Servants claimed they'd been instructed to pack his belongings during the night. Guards said they'd seen nothing. Eunuchs, who usually knew everything, suddenly developed collective amnesia.

Some said he'd left for Egypt, carrying letters of introduction to scholars in Alexandria. Others whispered he'd been eliminated quietly, his body burned without ceremony to avoid awkward questions.

A few claimed he still walked the upper corridors after midnight, barefoot and humming Syrian hymns—unable to leave, but no longer fully present.

I never learned the truth.

I kept the robe he'd left me—plain wool, travel-worn, smelling faintly of freedom. His final warning echoed in my mind: survival sometimes required vanishing before anyone noticed your predicament.

But I also knew that knowledge and action were different things. Understanding the cage didn't automatically open its door.

Some transformations had to be completed once begun.

Even if completion looked suspiciously like destruction.

The smart play was obvious—the same move Zoticus had made: disappear before the story reached its inevitable conclusion.

The problem was, I'd never been smart about knowing when to walk away from a race.

That's what had brought me here in the first place.

CHAPTER 8:

THE GIFT

"Imperial generosity was always a form of beautiful violence."

— Tacitus, Annals

Rome, 221 CE

She gave me a house.

Not just upgraded quarters or a promoted suite, but an actual domus—carved into the Palatine's slope like a jewel set in living rock. It had its own courtyard paved with lapis and pearl patterns, its own fountain pouring water into basins carved from single blocks of porphyry. Cypress trees lined the approach, dark spears pointing toward a sky that seemed bluer from these elevated windows.

"This is yours," Elagabalus said, tracing my shoulder with one finger. "Because you've forgotten how to want anything else."

At first, I couldn't trust it.

Her gifts were never simple rewards—they were stories she told about herself, evidence of her power to transform base materials into gold. But this gift was different. It wasn't public. It made no grand statement about imperial generosity.

She never even entered its doors.

That should have warned me.

The staff was entirely new, chosen by her household stewards: a cook whose tongue had been cut out years earlier for repeating palace gossip, a young servant who smelled perpetually of honey and moved with the careful precision of someone who'd learned sudden movements brought punishment, and an elderly woman who hummed while she worked—melodies that sounded familiar but belonged to no tradition I recognised.

None of them told me their names. They appeared when needed, vanished when not, and served with the efficiency of people who understood survival required invisibility.

The central courtyard held a single olive tree, ancient and gnarled, its branches trained into spiral patterns that must have taken decades to achieve.

I asked the humming woman if it had ever borne fruit.

She paused in her sweeping, considered the question seriously, then replied, "Only when no one's watching."

The first night I slept there, I woke in perfect darkness.

Not from dreams—rather, from the weight of silence. The kind that has substance, that presses against your eardrums and makes you aware of your own heartbeat.

I walked barefoot into the courtyard, the stones cool beneath my feet. The sky was a deep blue-black, just beginning to show the first promise of dawn.

She was there.

Standing beneath the olive tree, wearing nothing but moonlight and her own unbound hair, she looked less like an emperor than like something that had stepped from a tree's dreams into the waking world.

She did not acknowledge my presence, did not turn when I approached.

"Do you love it?" she asked the air.

"It isn't mine," I replied.

Now she turned, and in the uncertain light her smile was sharp as a knife.

"It is if you choose to stay."

Then she walked past me, gone before the first birds began their morning songs.

I began furnishing the house carefully, deliberately—a chair rescued from a palace storage room, a bowl filled with smooth river stones, a tapestry that had once hung behind the priestesses' seats, woven with constellations that belonged to no sky I recognised.

Slowly, it became more than a residence. It became a sanctuary.

Which was, I realised too late, exactly what made it dangerous.

Because a sanctuary can become a prison if someone else controls the key.

And I did not know the location of the hidden lock.

The gifts multiplied as summer deepened.

A comb carved from a single piece of mother-of-pearl. Shoes dyed with crushed orchids that stained my feet purple for days. An anklet strung with charms designed to ward off envy—a piece of jewellery that announced to everyone I was worth envying.

Each gift was more beautiful than the last. Each one another link in the chain I was helping to forge.

She never asked if I wanted them. Instead, she watched to see if I wore them, noted my choices, and adjusted her offerings accordingly.

Once, testing limits, I left a gift untouched.

It was a bronze serpent bracelet, its tail in its mouth—a symbol of eternity or entrapment, depending on perspective.

For three days, it sat on my shelf.

On the fourth day, she summoned me.

"You didn't care for it?" she asked, braiding her hair with movements that looked casual but revealed calculation in their precision.

"Didn't need it," I said carefully.

She nodded, as though this confirmed something important.

"Gifts aren't about need," she replied. "They're about remembering the giver."

That night, the bracelet vanished. In its place, she left a single thorn—rose or hawthorn, I couldn't tell. When I tried to pick it up, it drew blood.

I left it there for the rest of the year, a small altar to lessons learned.

The house began to change me—or perhaps it revealed changes already underway.

I became quieter, more contemplative. I learned to listen to the wind moving through stone, to birds that returned to the cypress trees only when human voices fell silent. I began writing again—short verses in scripts that looked familiar but belonged to no language I had formally learned.

I hid these writings beneath loose floor tiles in the westernmost room. Even the servants avoided that space, as though they sensed something undisturbed should remain so.

The senator's wife visited once—a woman who had known me slightly in my racing days, enough to claim old friendship when it served her purposes.

She admired the courtyard, complimented the fountain, and remarked on the quality of the marble with the expertise of someone who had priced many homes.

Then, lowering her voice, she said, "You must be very special to her."

I made a noncommittal sound.

She leaned closer, wine on her breath. "Be careful. She doesn't keep favourites long. She keeps relics."

After she left, I stood in the courtyard until the stars appeared, wondering what the house would become when I was gone. Who would they give it to? Would they convert it into a shrine, leave it empty as a monument to imperial whim, or let it be forgotten, like so many beautiful things that outlived their purpose?

A boy who smelled of honey brought me morning tea one day in late summer. He hesitated at the threshold, as if asking permission to speak.

"She sent something," he said finally.

The box was cedar, small enough to hold in cupped palms, perfumed with oils that made the air shimmer. Inside, wrapped in silk the colour of deep water, lay a mirror.

Not bronze, not glass, but polished silver that reflected light like captured stars.

I looked into it and saw my face—but not quite mine anymore. The features were the same, but something in their arrangement had shifted. The eyes held knowledge they hadn't possessed a year ago. The mouth suggested secrets it could not speak.

The mirror was the first to notice that I was becoming—or had already become—someone else.

The question was: was this transformation something I was choosing, or something that was happening to me?

In the racing world, you learned to tell the difference between controlling your speed and being carried by it.

This felt like being carried.

But the destination remained unclear.

CHAPTER 9:

THE FALL

"In the palace, decline comes not as storm but as silence: voices that no longer call your name, doors that no longer open at your approach."

— Court memoir, anonymous

Rome, 222 CE

The honey-scented boy vanished on a Tuesday.

One day he was there, bringing morning tea with his characteristic nervous precision, eyes downcast as always. The next, a different servant appeared: older, efficient, unremarkable. When I asked what had become of the boy, the new servant only shrugged.

"Reassigned," he said, as if that explained everything.

It was exactly how Zoticus had described his predecessor's departure. Not dramatic, not cruel, just a quiet redistribution of human resources when someone was no longer needed. The palace had an endless appetite for fresh faces and an equally efficient system for disposing of the used ones.

I should have recognised the warning signs earlier. But I had grown comfortable in my role, confident in my position, blind to the subtle shifts that marked the changing seasons of imperial favour.

Elagabalus's attention began to scatter.

Not withdrawn entirely; that would have been too blatant, too cruel even for her refined tastes. Instead, her attention was dispersed, divided, offered in smaller portions to a wider audience.

No more private dances. No more whispered jokes during ceremonies. No more gifts arriving with personal messages. Only presents that came unmarked, as if from anonymous admirers or perhaps the gods themselves.

I continued wearing the tunics, drinking the wine, and displaying the jewellery. But without her eyes to give them meaning, they became mere objects: beautiful, expensive, empty.

At court functions, I remained visible but unseen.

Senators turned their backs more freely, no longer calculating the cost of slighting me. Priests stepped aside from habit rather than reverence. A poet who had once begged for my attention now recited satire about "moths who mistake flame's heat for love's warmth."

I laughed louder than anyone, my amusement genuine because I could appreciate good craftsmanship even when it cut me.

But I left before the next verse could draw more blood.

The house remained mine. Another sign of how completely I had been forgotten.

If Elagabalus had truly cared about my fate, she would have reclaimed it. Redecorated it for her next project. Converted it into a mausoleum or a storage facility. Made some use of its beauty.

Instead, it stood unchanged, like a tomb waiting for its occupant to die.

I began walking the abandoned corridors at night.

Passages no longer lit by servants, halls where dust gathered in corners, and spider webs draped the spaces between columns like funeral shrouds. I traced mosaics with my fingertips, counting cracks that hadn't been there months before, noting which statues had developed new chips or stains.

In a disused temple chamber, I found an offering bowl overturned, its contents scattered across tiles no one had bothered to clean. Dried flowers and wine-stained bread, left to rot in forgotten corners.

The palace was forgetting itself as efficiently as it had forgotten me.

One evening, I heard familiar laughter echoing from behind silk curtains.

Elagabalus's laughter: low and intimate, edged with cruelty and sweetness in equal measure.

I didn't lift the curtain to see who shared her amusement now. I already knew what I would find: a new boy, golden and eager, learning the rhythms of imperial favour.

Learning what I was forgetting.

During rituals, I was repositioned further from the centre.

No longer holding the primary censer, but supporting torches. No longer leading invocations, but offering responses. Still present, still useful, but clearly secondary to newer, brighter flames.

When I stumbled over unfamiliar words, prayers I had once known perfectly, Elagabalus didn't correct me.

That was how I knew love had died: not through anger or punishment, but through indifference to my imperfections.

I tried to reclaim her attention with increasingly desperate gestures.

I wore the robe she had once said made me look like living fire. I sang the Syrian hymn that had moved her to tears during my first ritual. I danced the pattern she had taught me herself, each movement calculated to recall our shared intimacies.

She watched politely, as she might watch any competent performer.

Afterwards, she remarked, "The hymn sounds better in the original Greek."

I didn't speak Greek. I had never claimed to.

But her new favourite probably did.

One night, I waited outside her chambers for hours, hoping to intercept her before she retired. When the doors finally opened, it wasn't Elagabalus who emerged.

Golden boy paused when he saw me, and for a moment, his perfect composure cracked. I caught fear in his spring-water eyes. Not of me, but of time. Of the possibility that he might someday stand where I stood, outside doors that no longer opened for him.

He hurried past without speaking, silk slippers silent on the marble floors.

I understood then: I had become a cautionary tale.

When I returned to my house that night, the olive tree had shed all its leaves.

No wind had blown. No frost had fallen. The other trees in the courtyard remained green and healthy.

Only mine stood bare, its spiral branches naked against the starlight.

I swept the courtyard myself. The servants had stopped coming regularly. The fountain had run dry, the dolphins spilling nothing into empty basins. Even the replacement for the honey-scented boy had vanished, replaced by no one.

The following morning, a letter rested on my doorstep.

No seal, no signature, no indication of origin. Just three words, written in a script I almost recognised:

Be ready soon.

Neither warning nor invitation, neither threat nor promise. It might have been all of these.

Zoticus might have sent it, wherever he was.

Perhaps it came from myself, from the part of me that still remembered how to want freedom more than security.

I burned the letter without reading it again.

But I didn't sleep that night, or the night after.

Because I understood that even in a palace, all transformations eventually end.

The question was whether you chose the ending or waited for it to choose you.

And I had always been better at making the hard choice before the turn than waiting to see what happened.

It was time to remember who I used to be. Before the silk. Before the bells. Before the mirrors that showed me someone else's face.

Time to remember I was still, underneath it all, a charioteer.

And charioteers know when to pull the reins..

CHAPTER 10:

THE END

"The wise man leaves the feast while he can still walk."

— Syrian proverb

Rome, March 222 CE

It ended not with thunderclaps but with silence.

No riots in the streets. No daggers flashing in lamplight. No frantic messages racing through corridors like wildfire announcing the emperor's death.

Only the absence of sound where sound should have been—like a song cut short mid-note, the musicians suddenly forgetting they were playing.

I woke that final morning as I had every morning for four years: before dawn, bathed in water perfumed with oils I no longer noticed, and dressed in silk that had long since lost its strangeness.

But instead of the elaborate court robes, I chose a simple white tunic—the kind I had worn before titles and transformations, before gold and bells and chains made of beauty.

I braided my hair plainly, without ornaments.

I painted my face not at all.

Then I stepped into the courtyard, where the olive tree stood bare, its spiral branches dark against a sky that promised rain.

For the first time in months, the stones beneath my feet felt warm—like the earth itself remembered sunlight.

I packed nothing except my memory.

The robe Zoticus had left me: plain wool that smelled of honesty.

A scroll of proverbs I had never finished reading.

A silver mirror that had shown me faces I no longer recognised.

I wrapped these few things in an old cloak and left the bundle at the tree's base. Where I was going, I would not need reminders of what I had been.

The palace was quieter than I had ever known it.

For three days, rumours had spread through corridors like fever through a camp—letters from the Praetorian Guard, emergency sessions of senators who usually avoided one another, doors closed that had never been closed before.

Elagabalus had not appeared at the morning rites since the new moon. Even her most devoted priests could not explain her absence without their words sounding more like prayers than reasons.

The empire was holding its breath.

I walked toward the northern gate—the one used by servants and suppliers, the entrance that led through kitchen gardens and storage yards to the old road.

Two guards passed me without acknowledgement. Once, they would have bowed. Later, they would have nodded. Now they looked through me as if I were already gone.

That's how I knew I had permission to leave—not official permission, but the only kind that mattered in a place where everything was decided through gestures and omissions.

The gate stood unlocked.

I paused with my hand on the latch, not from fear but from something stranger—a moment of perfect stillness, as if the world had stopped spinning to let me choose my direction.

Then I opened it and stepped through.

No procession marked my departure. No farewells, no hands reaching to stop me. Just birdsong, the scent of earth after rain, and the sudden absence of a weight I hadn't realised I was carrying.

I made my way through the lower gardens, past cypress trees showing new growth, past wells where kitchen boys had once laughed, past statues of gods whose names I'd never bothered to learn because I thought I was becoming one myself.

Finally, I passed through the outer gate that opened onto the road leading away from Rome.

The stones were cracked the way old roads get when they're no longer important enough to repair. The air tasted of dust and possibility.

For the first time in two years, I breathed without counting the cost.

At the crest of the hill, I turned back once.

The palace spread below me like a golden mirage, still burning with morning light, still beautiful enough to stop the heart. From this distance, it looked like a temple, a mausoleum, or a stage waiting for the next tragedy to begin.

I thought of Elagabalus—of the way she touched my face that first day as if memorising it, of the moment she called me divine, of the last time she looked at me and saw nothing worth remembering.

I didn't curse her. I didn't thank her.

I simply let her go, the way you release a handful of sand to the wind.

The Empire was waiting with bated breath.

And me?

I walked until my legs ached and my palace-soft feet remembered what honest ground felt like. Walked until my name stopped following me in whispers, until my reflection surprised me with its ordinariness.

I found a coastal town where they needed someone who understood horses. When I said I had once driven chariots, they laughed—not with mockery, but with the genuine amusement of people who thought I was telling colourful lies.

They gave me work, a room above the stables, and bread that tasted of grain instead of ambition.

At night, I still dream of the Circus sometimes:

Sand between my teeth, reins cutting my palms, the crowd's roar washing over me like divine approval.

But I no longer dream of her.

That absence, more than anything, tells me I survived.

Occasionally, travellers bring news from Rome. They speak of a new emperor—steadier, more traditional, less interesting. They describe the Temple of the Sun, boarded shut and slowly crumbling. They tell stories of the boy-priest who once ruled as a god, who wore makeup, danced with fire, and vanished into myth.

They never mention me.

Which means I chose the right ending.

I still wear the ring Zoticus gave me—bronze, smooth, bearing no insignia except the weight of memory.

When people ask where I came from, I simply say, "The capital," then smile and change the subject.

Because there are stories that demand to be told, and truths that survive only in silence.

The truth is this: I left before they finished writing my story. I chose my own transformation, my own ending, my own return to something approaching human.

The finale lacked the drama poets prefer, but I owned it.

And in a world that tried to make me into myth, becoming human again was the most radical act of all.

A smart move would have been to stay, playing the game until it played itself out. But in those years, I had learned something that no silk or ceremony could touch:

Sometimes, the only way to win is to walk away from the track—

even if you never find out who crossed the finish line.

EPILOGUE

The letter arrives on a morning when the sea runs silver and the wind carries only salt instead of secrets.

I'm in the stables, as always at dawn, checking on a mare whose foal is due any day. Her breathing is steady, her eyes calm. She trusts me to know when something is wrong, and I've earned that trust through five years of arriving before sunrise, with gentle hands that never rush or demand.

The boy who delivers the letter—barely old enough to grow a beard—seems nervous. He asks three times if I'm truly the one called Hierocles, as if the name itself might be dangerous to speak.

"I was," I tell him. "Once."

The letter bears no seal, but I recognise the script immediately: careful, educated, with particular flourishes that mark Syrian training.

The one you loved is dead. They threw her body in the river like refuse, along with her mother. The Palace has been purged of Eastern influences. New gods. New customs. New emperor.

But I survived, as you did. As perhaps we all must, in our different ways.

If you wish to know more, there is a fishing boat that stops at your harbour on the new moon. Ask for the captain called Phoenix. He will have stories, if you want them.

If not, burn this letter and continue your good work with the horses. Some escapes should remain complete.

—A friend who remembers

I read it twice, then held it to the lamp flame. The papyrus catches quickly, curling into ash that I scatter from the window.

Some say she died within a week of my departure. They say she was dragged from her chambers by guards who had finally chosen a different emperor, thrown into the Tiber with her mother like failed statues toppled from their pedestals.

But I wasn't there to see it. I had already chosen my own path to freedom.

The boy-emperor who wore silk and kohl, who danced for Syrian gods, who tried to transform the empire's soul—reduced to a body in the river, a cautionary tale, a problem solved.

I should feel something. Grief, perhaps. Or relief. Or the bitter satisfaction of having chosen correctly when I walked away. Instead, I feel only the mild curiosity of someone hearing news about a place he used to live.

The new moon comes and goes. I don't seek out the fishing boat or the captain called Phoenix. Some stories are better left untold, some connections better left severed.

Instead, I help a mare birth her foal—a filly with her mother's steady temperament and her father's strong legs. She stands within the hour, nurses within two, and by evening is following her mother with the wobbling determination of all newborn things.

This seems more important than news from Rome.

That night, I dream of the Circus in the months to come. But it is not the old dream of falling, crashing, or reins that cut my hands bloody. Instead, I am simply standing in the sand, in the centre of that vast oval, with no horses, no chariot, no crowd to please or fear.

Just silence and space and the strange peace that comes from being exactly where you need to be.

When I wake, I remember feeling grateful. Not for what was, not for what might have been, but for what is: this small room above the stables, this life built from honest work, these hands that know the difference between a horse that trusts and one that merely obeys.

In the morning, the filly is strong enough to venture into the paddock. She explores her boundaries with careful steps, always returning to her mother's side when the world feels too large.

I watch her learn the shape of her small domain and think: this is what wisdom looks like. Not grand gestures of transformation, not a desperate reach for more than what you are, but patient mapping of what you have.

The sea continues its endless conversation with the shore. Horses require feed, water, and gentle attention. The sun rises and sets according to laws older than empires.

And I'm content to be a small part of these larger rhythms—to tend what needs tending, to exist without needing to become.

Years later, when travellers ask about my past, I tell them I used to work in the capital.

"Doing what?" they ask.

"Performing," I say.

They nod, as if this explains everything. Former entertainers are common enough—jugglers whose hands have lost their quickness, singers whose voices have cracked, dancers whose knees can no longer bear the strain of leaping.

They never press for details, and I never offer them.

Because the truth is too strange for casual conversation: that I was loved by someone who claimed to be divine, that I lived in a palace where truth was optional and identity a commodity, that I learned to become beautiful in ways that had nothing to do with who I actually was.

And that, in the end, the most radical thing I could do was remember how to be ordinary.

The filly grows strong and swift. By her second year, had shown promise as a riding horse—intelligent, willing, with a natural grace that can't be taught.

I could train her for racing. She has bloodlines, temperament, and a speed that makes crowds hold their breath.

Instead, I teach her to carry children safely, to respond to gentle guidance, to find joy in movement that serves rather than conquers.

She seems grateful for this smaller, kinder purpose.

As am I.

Sometimes, on clear nights when the stars emerge in patterns that once guided ceremonies I'd rather forget, I think about Elagabalus lying at the bottom of the Tiber.

Was she afraid in those final moments? Did she call for the gods who had spoken through her, or for the people who had failed to understand what she was trying to become?

Did she think of me?

Hope not. Hope her last thoughts were of flight, of transformation, of becoming something even death couldn't diminish.

She deserved a grander ending than the one Rome gave her.

But then again, perhaps we all do.

Horses never ask about my past. They know me by my touch, my voice, the way I move among them without hurry or aggression.

They've taught me that presence matters more than history, that trust is built in moments rather than years, that the most important transformations happen so gradually you don't notice them until they're complete.

I'm not the boy who drove chariots in the Circus.

I'm not the painted consort who danced in golden bells.

I'm the man who tends horses by the sea, who sleeps without nightmares, who has learned that freedom isn't the absence of chains but the presence of choice.

And if that's not the ending poets prefer—if it lacks the drama of death or the glory of revenge—then perhaps poets need to learn new stories.

Some victories are quiet.

Some transformations lead not upward but inward.

Some loves are best honoured with the courage to let them go.

The sea washes everything clean, in time.

Even memory.

Even myth.

Even the dreams of those who once danced with gods and lived to tell no one about it.

But in the end, I told someone after all.

I told the horses.

They're good listeners. Never judge. Never repeat what they hear.

The perfect audience for the kind of story that needs telling but doesn't need spreading.

And that's enough.

PYTHIAS

The Taster's Silence

PROLOGUE

I tasted everything—wine, words, and silences that held more poison than any cup.

For eight years, I stood in the shadow of the Roman Empire's strangest love story: the grieving emperor and the beautiful boy who died to become a god. I was invisible yet essential, trusted with Hadrian's life and his secrets.

History remembers Antinous as divine. It remembers Hadrian as a builder of walls and cities. It forgets the man who ensured the emperor lived long enough to transform murder into mythology.

That was my role: to taste what could kill, to hear what should never be spoken, to survive what others could never be allowed to witness.

Now, in a villa overlooking the sea, I tend grapes that will become honest wine. No one tests it for poison. No one whispers into cups or counts the cost of each breath.

But memory has its own weight, and some truths, once tasted, never fade.

I am the last living witness to how gods are made from grief, how love becomes possession, and how empire transforms everything it touches—even the truth.

The real story of what took place in those marble halls should be known.

Someone should taste the vintage before they drink the myth.

CHAPTER 1:

THE TASTER'S OATH

"Trust is the foundation of all service; in the palace, it is also its greatest danger."

— Pliny the Younger

Rome, 135 CE

They never poisoned Hadrian.

Or if they tried, I caught it.

That was my role. The tasting began early, detecting vinegar, spoiled meat, and the colour of a bruise under the wine. Then they taught me to read men's eyes: a servant's hesitation, a cup filled too quickly, a senator who smiled a moment too late.

I passed every test.

They said I had "the quiet"—silence, as if silence were inherited. What they meant was that I didn't flinch. Not when they fed me ink-thick goat's blood to simulate curdled wine. Not when I collapsed from nightshade, dosed just enough to prove a point. I spat once, got up, and asked if the next dose would be subtler.

Hadrian noticed that. Not the pain—the refusal to perform it.

He brought me from the kitchens to his inner court. Antinous was already there by then: the marble boy, the one who looked like a dream the gods had decided to remember.

I didn't envy him. Beauty is currency, and I'd seen what happened when debts came due.

What Hadrian wanted from me was different—someone who wouldn't leave traces. No rumours. No heirs. No cult.

I wasn't supposed to be remembered. That's why I survived.

The first time I tasted wine in front of him, I was fifteen.

He watched as I drank from his cup. Single swallow. Hold it. Wait. Breathe.

I closed my eyes. Five seconds. Ten. Still breathing.

I opened my eyes and said, "Safe."

He didn't nod. He just took the cup and sipped where my mouth had touched the rim. A ritual—an intimacy stranger than love.

Later that evening, he asked my name. I gave him the one I'd been sold under.

He shook his head. "No. That won't do. You're Greek, like him. But quieter."

He called me Pythias, after the oracle's mouthpiece at Delphi. A joke, I think. Or a prophecy.

Either way, I answered it from then on.

The training began years before that first cup.

They bought me from a trader in Nicomedia when I was twelve. A thin boy with quick hands and an unremarkable face that forgot itself—perfect for not being seen.

The head cook, a freedman named Marcus who had served three emperors, pointed to the corner where they kept the testing apparatus.

"You," he said. "Come."

Twenty small cups stood in careful rows, filled with various powders and liquids. Some harmless. Some not.

"Drink," Marcus ordered.

The first was water. Clean. The second, watered wine. Safe. The third burned. I gagged, but swallowed.

By the tenth cup, I was dizzy. By the fifteenth, my hands shook. The twentieth left everything tasting of copper for a week.

But I didn't die.

"You have tolerance," Marcus told me afterwards, while I lay sweating out whatever they had given me. "More important, you have discipline."

The training continued for three years. Every day brought something new: bitter almonds buried in honey cakes, the oily sheen of hemlock in dark wine, the way arsenic made fingernails feel soft.

They taught me to read the servants who prepared the food—how guilt showed in shoulders held too high, how fear made hands pour too slowly, how assassination looked different from accident, even when the poison was the same.

"We're not just detecting poison," Marcus explained. "We're detecting betrayal."

I learned other things too: how to be invisible in rooms full of important people, how to stand so still that conversations continued as if I weren't there, how to remember everything without appearing to listen.

How to survive proximity to power without being consumed by it.

People assumed I was a eunuch. I wasn't. But I learned not to correct them. It made things easier.

Antinous used to pass me in the halls and nod as though we shared something. We didn't. I knew his meals, his wine, and his dosage of fig syrup for headaches. I knew he hated fish oil candles. I knew how often he cried when Hadrian wasn't looking.

But I didn't know him.

He was the moon in our sky. I was the man who checked the ropes on the observatory.

Sometimes, during long evenings when Hadrian held court, I would watch them together—the emperor's hand on the boy's shoulder, Antinous laughing at jokes that weren't funny, the way they moved around each other like dancers who had rehearsed the same steps for years.

There was love there. Real love, I think. But it was performed as much as it was felt—every gesture calculated for the audience of courtiers and senators who watched for signs of favour or weakness.

My relationship with Hadrian was different. Private. Functional. Safe.

He trusted me because I wanted nothing from him except to keep him alive.

The oath we swore was never written down, not even spoken aloud. But I remember the words, because I told them to myself every day:

Taste everything. Trust nothing. Leave no trace.

That's how I kept him alive. That's how I stayed invisible. That's how I'm still here, long after the marble boy became a god and Hadrian became dust.

I write this not because I want to be remembered, but because someone should know what really happened in those halls. Someone should taste the truth.

The gods know I've swallowed worse things than poison.

CHAPTER 2:

THE BOY FROM BITHYNION

"Beauty draws the eye, but it is kindness that captures the heart."

— Greek proverb

Rome, 128 CE

He arrived on a Tuesday, during the rains.

I was in the kitchens testing the morning wine when the steward came down to tell us the emperor had acquired a new companion. A Greek boy, perhaps fourteen. Beautiful, they said from Bithynia.

I set down my cup and waited for the familiar tightness in my chest—the same province, the same rolling hills and olive groves I had left seven years earlier, when the tax collectors came for my father's farm.

"Pretty as a statue," the steward continued, warming his hands by the brazier. "Golden curls. Eyes like the sea. Hadrian saw him at some festival and decided he couldn't live without him."

Marcus caught my eye across the kitchen. He knew where I was from. Few people did.

"Well," he said carefully, "I suppose we'll be tasting for two now."

I saw Antinous for the first time three days later.

He was standing in the atrium, dripping wet from the baths, while a servant dried his hair. The late-afternoon light fell through the oculus above, turning him into something carved from gold and shadow.

The rumours hadn't lied. He was beautiful in a way that made you forget to breathe—but it went beyond that. He moved like someone who had never doubted his own worth, never questioned whether he belonged in whatever room he entered.

I had been invisible for so long that watching him was like looking at my opposite. He was everything I was not: noticed, desired, certain of his place.

He caught me watching and smiled—not the calculating smile I had learned to read on senators' faces, but something open and curious.

"You're new," he said.

"No," I replied. "You are."

He laughed at that—a sound like water over stones.

"I'm Antinous," he said, extending a hand still damp from the baths.

"Pythias."

We shook hands like equals, though we both knew we were not.

"From Bithynia," he said, tilting his head. A statement, not a question.

"How did you know?"

"The way you stand. We learn to be careful there. To watch the horizon."

He was right. Bithynia made you cautious. Too close to too many borders. Too many armies passing through. Too many ways for a small farm to vanish between one season and the next.

"Where in Bithynia?" I asked.

"Claudiopolis. My father had a tavern there," he said, then corrected himself. "Had. I suppose someone else runs it now."

"Mine had a farm. Olives, mostly. Near Nicomedia."

"Ah." He nodded, as though this explained something important. "So you know about waiting."

"Waiting?"

"For the rains to come. For the harvest to be good. For the tax collectors to pass you by." He wrapped the towel around his shoulders. "For your life to begin."

I had every intention of telling him that life didn't begin in places like this. It only changed shape—into something you no longer recognised. But he was looking at me with such hope that I couldn't bring myself to break it.

"Yes," I said instead. "I know about waiting."

Within a week, it was clear that Antinous wasn't just another pretty boy collected for the emperor's amusement.

Hadrian couldn't look away from him.

I watched it happen during the evening meals, standing against the wall with my silver cup, ready to taste whatever the emperor requested. Hadrian would be deep in conversation with his architects or philosophers—discussing the rebuilding of Athens or the movements of the stars—and then Antinous would shift in his chair or laugh at something someone said, and the emperor's attention would snap to him like a rope pulled taut.

It wasn't lust, exactly. Or not only lust. It was fascination. The way a scholar might study a text in an unknown language, convinced that if he stared long enough, its meaning would become clear.

Antinous seemed oblivious to the effect he had. He listened with genuine interest, asked thoughtful questions, and offered observations that showed he was cleverer than his beauty suggested. But he never preened, posed, or tried to hold Hadrian's attention the way others had.

That, of course, made Hadrian want him more.

I began to understand that I was watching something dangerous unfold. Not dangerous like poison—quick and certain. But dangerous like obsession: slow, consuming, impossible to cure once it took hold.

The other servants whispered about them.

"He's too young," the older ones said.

"He's too beautiful," said the cynical ones.

"He won't last," said those who had seen other favourites rise and fall.

But I could see what they couldn't. In the mornings, when I brought Hadrian his first cup of wine, I saw how the emperor's eyes had changed. Softer. More alive. As if something that had been sleeping for years had finally awakened.

And I saw how Antinous looked at Hadrian in return, not with the calculated affection of someone trying to secure his position, but with genuine warmth. The boy from Bithynia saw something in the emperor that the rest of us had forgotten was there.

A man, not just a god.

One evening, after a particularly long dinner, I was cleaning the wine cups when Antinous appeared in the kitchen.

"Couldn't sleep," he said, settling onto a stool beside the washing basin. "Too much wine, I think."

"I can make you something for that," I offered. "Mint tea with honey. It settles the stomach."

"Thank you."

I heated water over the brazier and prepared the tea while he watched. His presence filled the kitchen in a way mine never had. Even sitting quietly, he seemed to take up space, to matter.

"Do you miss it?" he asked suddenly.

"Miss what?"

"Home. Bithynia."

I considered the question while I stirred honey into his cup. Did I miss the farm—the backbreaking work, the constant worry about rain and taxes, about whether there would be enough grain to last the winter?

"I miss the quiet," I said finally. "The way you could walk for hours and see nothing but olive trees and sky."

"I miss the smell of bread baking," he said. "My father's tavern always smelled like bread and wine and woodsmoke. Simple things."

"Nothing here is simple."

He sipped his tea and nodded. "No. Everything means something else. Every word, every glance, every gesture. It's exhausting."

I almost smiled at that. He was learning.

"You'll get used to it," I said.

"Will I?" He looked at me with those impossible eyes. "Or will I become something else entirely?"

I didn't have an answer for that. I'd stopped being who I was so long ago I couldn't remember if the change had been gradual or sudden. One day, I was a farmer's son; the next, I was Pythias the taster. The person in between had simply disappeared.

"Does it matter?" I asked instead.

He was quiet for a long time. Then: "I hope so."

As the months passed, I watched Antinous navigate the court with growing skill. He learned which courtiers were worth cultivating and which were merely decorative. He discovered how to deflect unwanted attention without giving offence. He mastered the art of being charming without being threatening.

But more than that, he learned how to manage Hadrian's moods—how to coax the emperor out of his black periods with a well-timed joke or observation, how to listen to his theories about architecture or philosophy with just enough engagement to make him feel heard, how to be present without being demanding, available without being desperate.

It was a spectacle, subtly staged to resemble genuine affection. Maybe it was genuine affection. The line between the two blurred when survival depended on it.

I found myself admiring his skill even as I envied his position. He had what I would never have: the emperor's attention, the court's recognition, a place in the story being written around us.

But I also saw what that attention cost him—the careful calculation behind every seemingly spontaneous gesture, the way he shaped himself to Hadrian's needs, smoothing away the rough edges of his own personality until only the parts the emperor wanted remained visible.

We were both from Bithynia. We had both been chosen for service. But where I had learned to disappear, Antinous had learned to shine.

I wondered which of us would survive longer.

I wondered which of us was already dead.

One night, as I was preparing Hadrian's bedtime wine, I found Antinous standing on the balcony overlooking the city. The torches below flickered like fallen stars.

"Do you ever think about going back?" he asked without turning around.

"To Bithynia?"

"To who we were before."

I joined him at the railing. The night air was cool, touched with the scent of jasmine from the gardens below.

"I think about it," I said. "But I'm not sure there's anything to go back to."

"No." He was quiet for a moment. "I got a letter last month from my father. He's remarried. Has a new son. Named him Antinous."

"After you."

"After the dead one. The son who left for Rome and never came home."

I wanted to tell him he wasn't dead—that he was more alive than most people in this palace, more real than the marble statues that filled its halls. But I could see in his face that he already knew the truth.

The boy from Bithynia was gone. What remained was Antinous, the emperor's beloved. Beautiful. Perfect. Untouchable.

And like all perfect things, destined to break.

"I should go," he said, stepping back from the railing. "Hadrian will be wondering where I am."

I watched him walk away, this golden boy who shared my past but not my future. In a few years, artists would carve his face in marble, poets would write hymns in his honour, and priests would offer sacrifices at his altar.

But tonight, he was just a homesick boy from a tavern in Claudiopolis, pretending to be someone else.

Tomorrow, I will taste Hadrian's wine and ensure he lives another day.

And the empire would turn on its axis, grinding us all to dust beneath its wheel.

Some of us just took longer to disappear than others.

CHAPTER 3:

THE EMPEROR'S SHADOW

"The wise servant hears all, sees all, and remembers what his master would forget."

— Palace wisdom, attributed to various courts

Rome, 129 CE

It took months for Hadrian to trust me with more than wine. First came the messages I was meant to forget. Then the private correspondence I wasn't supposed to understand. Finally, the midnight summons began—not for poison detection, but for something rarer: honest conversation.

Hadrian never slept well.

I knew this before Antinous did, before the courtiers who tracked the emperor's moods for signs of political weather. I knew because I was the one who brought him warm wine at midnight when his mind would not quiet, the one who stood in the doorway while he paced and muttered about aqueducts, star charts, and the rebellious tribes beyond the wall he was building in Britain.

"Taste," he would say, gesturing absently at the cup. Not because he feared poison at that hour, but because the ritual soothed him—the familiar motion of cup to lip, the pause, the nod. A constant in a world where everything else shifted like sand.

In public, Hadrian was marble—controlled, divine. The gods spoke through him, the architects said. His vision shaped stone into perfection, transformed cities into monuments to Roman order.

In private, at three in the morning, he was just a man who could not stop thinking.

"Do you know what Alexander did wrong?" he asked me one night, six months after Antinous had arrived.

I was testing wine that had gone slightly sour—not dangerous, but unpleasant. "No, Caesar."

"He died too young." Hadrian stood at his window, looking out over the city. "Thirty-two years old. Can you imagine? All that power, all that potential, and he couldn't even live long enough to see what he had built."

"Perhaps that's why he's remembered as great," I said carefully. "He died before he could disappoint anyone."

Hadrian turned to look at me. In the lamplight, his face seemed older than his fifty-three years.

"You think I disappoint people?"

"I think you're still alive to try again when you do."

He almost smiled at that.

"Spoken like a true cynic."

"Spoken like someone who tastes your food, Caesar. I have a vested interest in keeping you breathing."

That time, he did smile. His composure rarely cracked, but sometimes amusement showed itself in those private moments.

"Tell me about your dreams," he said suddenly.

"My dreams?"

"When you sleep. Do you dream of Bithynia? Of the life you might have had?"

The question caught me off guard. Hadrian rarely asked about my past, content to treat me as a fixture of his court rather than a person with history.

"Sometimes," I admitted.

"What do you see?"

I considered lying—offering him some pastoral fantasy of sheep and olive groves. But something in his voice compelled honesty.

"I dream I'm still twelve years old," I said. "Standing in my father's house while strangers count our belongings. I dream I'm trying to tell them that the farm isn't worth what they think it is—that the soil is rocky, and the well runs dry in summer. But they can't hear me."

Hadrian nodded slowly. "I dream I'm building a wall," he said. "But no matter how high I make it, there's always something on the other side trying to get through. And I can never see what it is."

We stood in comfortable silence, two men sharing the peculiar intimacy of insomnia.

"Does Antinous know you don't sleep?" I asked.

"Antinous sleeps like the dead," Hadrian said, and there was something almost wistful in his voice. "He closes his eyes and disappears. I envy that."

"Youth," I said.

"Innocence," he corrected. "The ability to trust that tomorrow will be better than today."

"Do you trust that?"

He looked at me steadily for some time. "I trust that you'll taste my wine tomorrow morning. And that if there's poison in it, you'll be the one who dies."

His words lacked cruelty—just matter-of-fact, a statement of the order of things.

"Yes, Caesar," I said.

"Good." He returned to his window. "That's the only certainty I need."

The pattern established itself over the following months. Days belonged to the public. Hadrian, the emperor who held court, received ambassadors and reviewed architectural plans and military reports. Evenings belonged to Antinous—dinners, conversations, and the kind of attention that made the beautiful boy glow like a flame.

But the hours between midnight and dawn belonged to me.

Hadrian would summon me with a gesture or a word to a servant. I would appear with wine and my silver cup, and we would enact our familiar ritual. Sometimes he wanted to talk.

Sometimes he wanted silence. Always, he wanted the reassurance that someone was awake with him in the vast loneliness of power.

"I'm thinking of moving the capital," he told me one night in late autumn.

"Where?"

"Athens. Or Alexandria. Somewhere with proper libraries. Rome feels..." He gestured vaguely at the surrounding walls. "Old. Tired. Built by men who thought the world ended at the Rhine."

"The Senate would object."

"The Senate objects to everything." He sipped his wine, noting its quality with the absent attention of a man for whom excellence was expected. "What do you think? Could a Greek boy from Bithynia be happy in Athens?"

I understood he wasn't talking about me.

"I think Greek boys adapt," I said. "We learn to be happy wherever we're useful."

"Useful." He repeated the word as if tasting it. "Is that what you call yourself?"

"It's what I am."

"And Antinous? What is he?"

The question hung in the air between us. I knew what Hadrian wanted me to say—that Antinous was beloved, treasured, irreplaceable. But late-night conversations had their own rules, different from the daylight world of ceremony and flattery.

"He's beautiful," I said finally.

"Yes."

"Beauty doesn't last."

"No." Hadrian set down his cup and turned his eyes to me. "But neither does usefulness."

"Usefulness lasts longer."

"Does it?" He moved to his desk, where scrolls lay scattered like fallen leaves. "I have architects who are useful. Engineers. Generals. All indispensable until someone younger and cleverer comes along. But beauty..." He lifted a scroll and let it fall again. "Beauty burns itself into memory. Lasts longer than marble."

"Memory can be edited, Caesar."

"Can it?"

"History is written by whoever survives longest."

He was quiet for so long, I thought he had forgotten I was there. Then:

"And you plan to survive, don't you, Pythias?"

"It's what I'm trained for."

"Yes." He returned to the window. "Sometimes I think you're the only honest man in Rome."

"I'm not honest, Caesar. I'm careful."

"Same thing, in the end."

Winter brought news from the provinces: unrest in Judaea, problems with the grain supply from Egypt, reports of strange omens in the sky above Dacia.

Hadrian grew more restless. The midnight conversations became longer, more frequent. He would pace while I stood motionless against the wall, cup ready, watching him wear grooves in the marble floor.

"Do you believe in omens?" he asked one night during the Saturnalia celebrations. Outside, the city was drunk and singing. Inside, we maintained our familiar quiet.

"I believe in patterns," I said.

"Meaning?"

"Birds flying south mean winter is coming. Servants whispering means someone is planning betrayal. Emperors asking about omens mean they're worried about something they can't control."

He stopped pacing. "And what am I worried about?"

The honest answer was everything. The borders were unstable. The treasury was strained from his building projects. The Senate tolerated him but didn't love him. The people respected him, but didn't worship him the way they had Augustus.

But beneath all that was something simpler, more immediate.

"You're worried about time," I said.

"Time?"

"You're fifty-four, Caesar. Alexander conquered the world by thirty. You're wondering what you'll be remembered for."

"And?"

"You're wondering if love is enough."

The words hung between us like smoke. I thought I had gone too far, crossed some invisible line that separated honest counsel from dangerous presumption.

But Hadrian only nodded.

"He's so young," he said quietly.

"Yes."

"I look at him and see..." He stopped, then began again. "Do you know what it's like to love something that will outlive you?"

"No, Caesar."

"It's terrifying. And wonderful. And absolutely necessary." He looked at me. "You'll understand someday."

I wanted to tell him I understood already—that I had been watching him love Antinous for over a year, seeing how it transformed him and terrified him in equal measure. That I had been taking notes, in my way, recording the small daily erosions and revelations no historian would ever document.

But that wasn't my role. My role was to listen. To taste. To remain.

"More wine, Caesar?"

"Yes. But taste it carefully. I have a feeling the new year will bring changes."

I lifted the cup to my lips, held the wine on my tongue, and waited for my body to tell me what it contained.

Salt. Honey. The ghost of poppies.

And beneath it all, the faint metallic taste that meant someone, somewhere, was afraid.

"Safe," I said, passing him the cup.

He drank from the place where I'd sipped—our nightly communion of trust and survival.

Outside, the city celebrated. Inside, an emperor worried about time, and a slave planned to outlive them all.

Some intimacies are too complex for history to record.

This was one of them.

CHAPTER 4:

EGYPT

"The gods of the Nile demand sacrifice; the question is always who will pay the price."

— Herodotus

The Nile, 130 CE

Egypt changed everything.

The journey down from Alexandria began pleasantly enough—barges loaded with wine and cushions, priests greeting us at every temple. But the river itself felt different. Older. It moved with the weight of centuries, carrying silt and secrets in equal measure.

Gods were dangerous things to travel with.

Hadrian grew restless as we moved south. The midnight wine sessions became erratic—sometimes lasting until dawn, sometimes skipped entirely when he disappeared into the forward cabin with maps and scrolls.

"He's planning something," Antinous said to me one morning as we watched the emperor pace the deck.

"He's always planning something."

"Not like this." Antinous's voice was careful. "He's been asking me about dreams."

"What kind of dreams?"

"Strange ones. About stars falling into the river. About cities sinking beneath the sand." Antinous touched the rail, his fingers drumming nervously. "He asks if I've ever dreamed of dying."

Something cold settled in my stomach. "What do you tell him?"

"That I dream of home sometimes. Of bread baking and my father's voice calling me for dinner." He looked at me. "Normal dreams. Boring dreams."

"Good."

"Is it?" He turned to face me fully. "Pythias, what do you know about Egyptian religion?"

"Very little. Why?"

"The priests who came aboard yesterday. They kept looking at me. Not the way people usually look. Different. Like they were seeing something else."

I remembered them—three old men with shaved heads and eyes that seemed to hold too much knowledge. They had spoken briefly with Hadrian in Greek, then retreated to burn incense and mutter prayers in their ancient tongue.

"Priests see omens everywhere," I said. "It's their profession."

"Maybe." But Antinous didn't sound convinced.

We reached Hermopolis on a day when the wind died and the river moved like oil. The local governor greeted us with gifts, but it was the high priest who captured Hadrian's attention—a thin man with intelligent eyes and hands stained purple from handling sacred texts.

"Welcome to the city of Thoth," he said in accented Greek. "The god of wisdom has been expecting you."

"Has he?" Hadrian's voice carried dry amusement.

"The stars have been… active. Much movement in the house of transformation." The priest's gaze flicked briefly to Antinous, then away. "Perhaps the Caesar would honour us by consulting the sacred texts? We have scrolls that speak of the destiny of kings."

I watched Hadrian's face change. The amusement faded, replaced by something hungrier.

"Show me," he said.

They brought us to a temple carved into the hillside. Inside, oil lamps flickered like captured stars. The walls were covered in hieroglyphs that seemed to shift when you weren't looking directly at them.

The priest led us to a chamber where scrolls lay unrolled on a low table—papyrus covered in symbols I couldn't read, their age unmistakable.

"Here," the priest said, pointing to a section decorated with painted figures. "The prophecy of the divine youth."

Hadrian leaned closer. "Tell me."

"When the river runs backwards and the dead walk among the living, a beautiful one shall join the gods through water and transformation. His sacrifice shall ensure the immortality of the one who loves him."

The words fell into the chamber like stones into a well. In the silence that followed, I could hear my own heartbeat.

"And this prophecy," Hadrian said carefully, "when was it written?"

"In the time of the first pharaohs, Caesar—before your Rome was even imagined."

I glanced at Antinous. His face had gone pale, but he stood motionless, trained not to react to dangerous words.

"Interesting," Hadrian said at last. "Are there other interpretations?"

The priest smiled. "There are always other interpretations, Caesar. The gods speak in riddles so that mortals might exercise their wisdom in understanding."

But I could see in Hadrian's eyes that he had already chosen his interpretation.

That night, I was summoned to his cabin earlier than usual. The wine I brought was stronger than normal—Falernian mixed with something that made the air taste of copper and strange spices.

"Taste," he said absently, his attention fixed on a scroll spread across his desk.

I sipped. The wine was clean, but beneath it I detected something herbal—something that quickened the pulse and sharpened the mind.

"What did you think of the priest's words?" Hadrian asked without looking up.

"I think priests say what they believe their audience wants to hear."

"Do they?" He finally looked at me. His pupils were dilated. "And what does this audience want to hear?"

I chose my words carefully. "That the gods have a plan. That death has meaning. That love can conquer time."

"Yes." He returned to the scroll. "All true things, in their way."

"Caesar—"

"Do you know what this is?" He gestured at the papyrus. "A map of the afterlife. The Egyptians believe death is just another journey."

"And you believe this?"

"I believe in transformation." He rolled up the scroll with steady hands. "Love so pure it changes the fundamental nature of existence."

The wine I had tasted was making my head light—or perhaps his words were venom, a kind of poison.

"Antinous is troubled," I said.

Antinous is young. The young always trouble themselves with things beyond their understanding."

"What if he's right to be troubled?"

Hadrian looked at me for a long moment. "Are you questioning my judgement, Pythias?"

"I'm questioning whether love should require sacrifice."

"All love requires sacrifice." He stood and moved to the window, where the Nile reflected the stars. "The question is whether the sacrifice has meaning."

I wanted to argue, but I had learned there were conversations I could have with Hadrian—and conversations that would end with my death.

This was the second kind.

"More wine, Caesar?"

"No. But stay. I don't want to be alone with my thoughts tonight."

So I stood against the wall, watching an emperor plan something that would echo through history. Outside, the river flowed north toward the sea, carrying its burden of silt and dreams toward an uncertain delta.

By morning, Antinous was gone.

The search began at once. I found the first clue an hour after dawn—wet footprints leading from his cabin to the deck, then stopping at the rail.

"He went into the water," I told Hadrian.

"I can see that." His voice was steady, but his hands gripped the rail until his knuckles whitened. "The question is whether he jumped or was pushed."

I thought of the priest's prophecy, of the scroll Hadrian had studied so intently, of the strange herbal taste in last night's wine.

"Does it matter?" I asked.

His gaze betrayed no surprise, only a terrible kind of satisfaction.

"No," he said quietly. "It doesn't matter at all."

The Nile flowed on, indifferent to our grief and guilt, carrying its long memory toward the sea.

By evening, they had found the body.

By the next morning, they were already planning the temples.

CHAPTER 5:

THE STILL CUP

"Grief shared becomes lighter; grief hidden becomes poison."
— Euripides

Hermopolis, 130 CE

The wine tasted of grief.

Not literally—grief has no flavour, whatever the poets claim. Yet the cup Hadrian pressed to his lips that morning carried something wrong. Not poison. Stillness. As if the liquid itself had forgotten how to move.

"Taste," he said, though his voice was barely a whisper.

I lifted the cup. The wine was Lesbian, pale gold—the kind reserved for celebrations. But when it touched my tongue, I felt nothing. No warmth, no bite, no life. Just liquid that had given up hope.

"Safe," I said, because it was true in the only way that mattered anymore.

Hadrian drank without pleasure, without ceremony. The man who had once turned dining into art now consumed food like medicine—necessary, joyless, forgotten the moment it was swallowed.

"They want to build a city," he said suddenly.

"Caesar?"

"The priests. The governor. They say the spot where he… where it happened… is sacred now. They want to build a city around it. Antinoöpolis." He spoke the name as if testing poison. "A place for pilgrims to come and remember."

I said nothing. What was there to say? That cities built on grief often outlast the sorrow that created them? Was that marble easier to worship than memory?

"They've prepared the scrolls," he continued. "The official account. Would you like to hear it?"

I nodded, though I already knew what it would contain.

"Antinous, beloved companion of Caesar, while travelling the sacred Nile, was seized by divine inspiration and offered himself to the river gods to ensure the continued prosperity of the empire and the health of the emperor. His noble sacrifice was witnessed by priests of the temple of Thoth, who confirmed the sacred nature of his transformation."

The words fell like stones into still water.

"Very poetic," I said.

"Yes. The scribes worked all night. Amazing how quickly tragedy becomes legend when you have the right words." He set down his cup. "Burn them."

"Caesar?"

"The real scrolls. The priest's prophecy. My notes. The correspondence with the temple astronomers. All of it. I want them burned."

"Wouldn't it be simpler to—"

"Burn them yourself. I trust your discretion."

I understood. He didn't want servants who might be questioned later. He didn't want evidence that could be traced, interpreted, or used against him. He wanted the truth to disappear, leaving only the beautiful lie.

"Yes, Caesar."

"And Pythias?" He looked at me with eyes I had no desire to explore. "Thank you. For your service. For your silence."

It was not a request. It was a reminder of what my survival depended on.

I burned the scrolls at dawn, in a brazier set up in the garden of the governor's residence. The papyrus caught quickly—millennia of accumulated wisdom reduced to ash in minutes.

But I read them first.

The priest's prophecy was older than he had claimed, though not as ancient as he had implied. Written during the reign of Ptolemy II, when the old kingdom was already fading into Rome's shadow. The star charts were recent commissioned by Hadrian himself, tracing the movement of celestial bodies through what the Egyptians called the "house of transformation."

And then there were Hadrian's own notes: page after page of calculations, correspondences with augurs and astrologers, sketches of temple layouts and ceremonial designs. Plans within plans, all leading to the same conclusion.

The emperor had not simply allowed Antinous to die. He had orchestrated it.

As the flames consumed the evidence, something shifted inside me. Not anger—that was too dangerous, too useless. But clarity. For months, I had thought I was watching love destroy itself through obsession.

Instead, I had been watching love transform into something else entirely. Something that could kill what it claimed to cherish, all for the promise of preserving it forever.

The ashes scattered on the morning wind, carrying their secrets toward the Nile.

The whispers began that afternoon.

Servants who had been with us on the barge, speaking in voices they thought private. Soldiers who had searched the waters, comparing stories that didn't quite match. Local priests who had seen the body when it was pulled from the river.

"Marks on his wrists," one said.

"Bruise on his temple," said another.

"But the priests said—"

"The priests say what they're paid to say."

I listened without seeming to listen. I tasted wine without comment. I stood in shadows while truth tried to surface, like bodies in dark water.

By evening, the whispers had reached the palace. I found Hadrian in his study, surrounded by architects' drawings for the new city. His hand was steady as he traced lines on papyrus, marking out streets, temples, and monuments.

"They're talking," I said quietly.

"Are they?" He didn't look up from his work. "What are they saying?"

"That Antinous didn't go into the water willingly."

"Grief makes people imaginative. They see conspiracy where there is only tragedy." He selected a different stylus and began adding details to a temple façade. "Of course, imagination can be dangerous. Perhaps some of the more talkative servants should be reassigned—sent somewhere distant, quiet."

I understood. The witnesses were disappearing one by one—transferred to other provinces, given new assignments, or placed in positions that kept them far from anyone who might ask inconvenient questions.

"And the soldiers who searched?"

"Heroes who tried valiantly to save a drowning companion. They'll be rewarded, promoted, given reason to remember their loyalty rather than their doubts."

"And the priests?"

"The priests have seen a miracle—divine transformation. They'll spend the rest of their lives explaining its significance to pilgrims." He finally looked up. "Everyone gets what they want, Pythias. The servants get new positions, the soldiers get advancement, and the priests get a cult to administer. And I get..."

He didn't finish the sentence.

"What do you get, Caesar?"

"Immortality." He returned to his drawing. "In six months, there will be temples from here to Britain where pilgrims offer prayers to the divine Antinous. In ten years, there will be statues in every city of the empire. In a hundred years, there will be stories."

"And in a thousand years?"

"In a thousand years, no one will remember how he died—only that he loved an emperor enough to become a god."

I watched him work, adding careful lines to structures that would outlast everyone in that room. Outside, the Nile flowed toward its delta, carrying both silt and secrets.

"Will you visit the temples?" I asked.

"Of course. It would be impious not to honour the divine Antinous." He spoke the name without irony, as if he had already forgotten the boy from Bithynia who used to cry when Hadrian wasn't looking. "Will you accompany me?"

"If you require it, Caesar."

"I require very little these days. Food, wine, someone to ensure neither is poisoned." He set down his stylus. "Do you think less of me, Pythias?"

The question surprised me. I had expected many things, but not this moment of what might have been vulnerability.

"I think you loved him," I said carefully.

"That's not what I asked."

I considered my answer. In the morning, I would taste his wine to ensure he survived another day. In the evening, I would stand in shadows while he received reports from across the empire. In the long years ahead, I would watch him build monuments to justify what had happened on the Nile.

"I think you did what emperors do," I said finally. "You transformed love into power."

He nodded, as if I had confirmed something he already knew. "Then we understand each other."

"Yes, Caesar."

"Good. Pour the wine. I find I'm thirsty."

I lifted the cup, tasted liquid that moved like grief, and pronounced it safe.

Outside, workmen were already breaking ground for the first temple.

Inside, an emperor drank wine that tasted of memory and planned his own immortality.

And in the space between truth and legend, a boy from Bithynia began his transformation into something that would outlast bronze, marble, and the men who claimed to love him.

Some sacrifices feed the gods.

Others feed the people who make them.

CHAPTER 6:

A GOD INVENTED

"Men make gods in their own image, then worship what they have created."

— Xenophanes

Rome, 131 CE

The first statue arrived on a Tuesday, wrapped in silk and carried by six slaves who moved as though they bore a body to burial.

I watched from the colonnade as they unwrapped it in the atrium: white marble, perfectly carved, capturing Antinous at seventeen with the impossible beauty that had made an emperor forget himself. The artist had smoothed away the small imperfections I remembered—the scar on his chin from a childhood fall, the faint asymmetry of his smile when he was thinking.

This was Antinous as the gods would remember him: perfect, eternal. Nothing like the boy who once asked me for mint tea when he couldn't sleep.

"Beautiful work," Hadrian said, running his fingers along the marble cheek. "The sculptor studied the preparatory sketches carefully. Every detail is authentic."

"Yes, Caesar."

"Place it in the eastern garden, where the morning light will touch it first."

The slaves carried their burden away, and I wondered whether any of them had known the living boy—if they felt the strange weight of moving someone they had once served, transformed now into stone and worship.

"The coins are ready as well," Hadrian continued, producing a small silver disc from his toga. "The mint has been working day and night."

I examined the coin. On one side was Hadrian's profile with the familiar inscription: HADRIANVS AVGVSTVS. On the reverse, Antinous's face, surrounded by the words ANTINOOS HERO.

Hero. Not yet a god. That would come later, as the cult spread, grew, and demanded more elaborate justifications.

"The first issues go to Alexandria," Hadrian said. "Then Athens, Ephesus, and the other Greek cities. People who understand the connection between beauty and divinity."

"And Rome?"

"Rome will learn to understand." He pocketed the coin. "The Senate has already approved the temple construction. Amazing how cooperative they become when devotion is framed as imperial policy."

The letters began arriving within the month—governors seeking guidance on ritual observances, priests requesting clarification on feast days and sacrifices, architects submitting plans for temples, theatres, gymnasiums to be built in the new god's honour.

I read them all in my capacity as keeper of Hadrian's correspondence. My literacy was one of the reasons I survived the transition from kitchen slave to imperial confidant—for few trusted someone who could read their secrets.

> *From the Governor of Bithynia: The people of Claudiopolis have petitioned to rename their city Antinoöpolis Minor in honour of their divine son. They also request permission to mint local coins bearing his image and to establish annual games in his memory.*
> *From the High Priest of Apollo at Delphi: The Oracle has spoken favourably of including the divine Antinous in our sacred mysteries. We seek guidance on the appropriate epithets and ritual forms.*
> *From the Procurator of Egypt: Construction proceeds rapidly on the new city. The temple foundation has been blessed by the priests of Thoth, Osiris, and Serapis. Local workers report miraculous signs—lotus flowers blooming out of season and the Nile flowing more sweetly near the sacred site.*

Each letter was answered carefully, with Hadrian dictating responses that wove together Greek theology, Egyptian mysticism, and Roman administrative efficiency. Antinous was becoming Osiris-Antinous, Apollo-Antinous, Bacchus-Antinous. Every city found a way to fit him into its existing pantheon.

"The key," Hadrian explained as I transcribed yet another theological ruling, "is to let each place see him as it needs him to be: a hunter to the Arcadians, a poet to the Athenians, a beloved youth to those who remember what it was to be young."

"And to you, Caesar? What is he to you?"

Hadrian paused in his dictation. Outside, I could hear workmen in the garden, preparing the ground for another statue—this one in Egyptian style, with the divine uraeus and the nemes headdress.

"To me, he is proof that love can transcend death," he said finally. "That what we cherish can be preserved, if we're willing to pay the price."

I wrote down his words, though they weren't meant for the letter. Some truths escaped even when you tried to contain them.

The festivals began in spring.

Antinoia—celebrations held across the empire on the anniversary of his death, or his transformation, as the official proclamations described it: games, sacrifices, theatrical displays, mystery rites conducted by priests who had never known the living boy but who spoke of his divine nature with absolute conviction.

I attended the first one held in Rome, standing at Hadrian's side as citizens who had never heard of Antinous six months earlier offered prayers for his intercession. Young men crowned with flowers competed in races and wrestling matches. Poets recited verses comparing him to Ganymede, to Hyacinthus, to all the beautiful boys the gods had loved and claimed.

"Does it feel strange?" I asked quietly as we watched a group of acolytes perform a dance supposedly revealed to them in dreams.

"Does what feel strange?"

"Watching people worship someone you knew. Someone who used to complain about the weather and ask for honey cakes after dinner."

Hadrian was quiet for what felt like forever; I thought he wouldn't answer. Then: "I don't watch them worship Antinous. I watch them worship what Antinous became."

"And what did he become?"

"Everything he was always meant to be. Beautiful. Beloved. Eternal."

The dancers spun faster, their movements growing more frenzied as the drums accelerated. Several collapsed, claiming divine possession. The crowd pressed forward, reaching out to touch them, hoping some of the god's presence might pass through contact.

"He would have laughed at this," I said.

"Would he?" Hadrian's voice carried a warning. "How can you know what the divine Antinous would have thought? You only knew the mortal boy."

I understood. The living Antinous was becoming inconvenient to the myth. His actual personality—his doubts, fears, and homesickness—had to be erased to make room for the perfect beloved the empire needed him to be.

History was being rewritten in real time, and I was one of the few people left who remembered the original text.

That night, I began my own chronicle.

Not the official version that would survive in imperial archives. Not the theological treatises that would justify his cult to future generations. Just facts, recorded in the plain Greek I had learned in the kitchens, hidden in a scroll I kept beneath my sleeping mat.

His name was Antinous. He came from Claudiopolis in Bithynia. He was fourteen when he arrived at court, nineteen when he died. He liked honey cakes and often complained of headaches. He missed his father's tavern. He was beautiful, but he was also kind—which is rarer and more valuable than beauty.

The emperor loved him. I believe that love was real. But love and murder can exist in the same heart when the lover values possession more than the beloved's life.

They say he threw himself into the Nile to save Hadrian's life. They say the gods called him to transformation. They say many things that are not true.

I say this: he died afraid. I say this: he did not choose his death. I say this: the god they worship is not the boy I knew.

I wrote by lamplight, in characters small enough to fit lifetimes onto single sheets of papyrus. When I finished each section, I rolled it carefully and sealed it with wax that bore no identifying marks.

I didn't know who would ever read these words. Perhaps no one. Perhaps some future scholar, centuries hence, will be trying to separate myth from history. Perhaps it didn't matter.

What mattered was that someone had written it down. That somewhere, in some forgotten archive or buried cache, the truth would survive.

The gods they were building temples to deserved better than the lies that created them.

And the boy from Bithynia deserved to be remembered as he actually was: flawed, mortal, afraid, and human.

Even gods had once been human.

Especially gods.

The last entry I made that first night was the simplest:

I was there. I saw. I tasted his tears in the wine I tested, heard his prayers when he thought no one was listening. His fear was real. His death was not voluntary. His transformation into divinity serves purposes he would not have chosen.

But his kindness was also real. His laughter. His homesickness for a place that exists now only in memory.

They can carve his face in marble and mint his image on coins. They can build temples and write hymns and train priests to perform mysteries in his name.

They cannot touch what I remember.

That belongs to me.

I sealed the scroll and hid it carefully. Outside, the night was quiet, broken only by the distant sounds of celebration drifting from the taverns, where citizens—drunk on wine and newly minted mythology—sang hymns to gods they had invented that very afternoon.

Tomorrow, I will taste Hadrian's breakfast wine and ensure he lives to see another day of his immortality project.

Tonight, I kept my own vigil for the dead.

CHAPTER 7:

THE WINTER PALACE

"Age teaches emperors what youth never could: that even gods grow weary."

— Marcus Aurelius, Meditations

Rome, 136 CE

The emperor's hands shook when he assumed no one was watching.

I noticed it first during the wine ritual—the slight tremor as he lifted the cup, the way he had to concentrate to keep the liquid from spilling. Then I saw it when he signed documents, when he gestured during audiences, when he thought himself alone and unobserved.

Hadrian was dying. Not quickly, not dramatically, but with the persistence of a body tired of shouldering the empire's weight.

"The physicians say it's nothing," he told me one evening as I helped him to his chair. His legs had given out halfway across the study, and for a moment I had seen terror flash across his face—not of death, but of weakness witnessed.

"The physicians say many things, Caesar."

"Yes. Most of them are designed to make me feel better about the inevitable." He settled into the chair with the careful movements of someone whose bones had begun to betray him. "How long do you think I have?"

The question was asked casually, as if inquiring about the weather. But I had learned to read the subtle signs of imperial distress: the tightness around his eyes, the way his breathing grew shallow when he was afraid.

"Longer than most men," I said. "Less time than you want."

"Always honest, aren't you, Pythias?"

"It's what you pay me for."

"Is it?" He gave me a look that seemed older than his sixty years. "I thought I paid you to keep me alive."

"I can't keep you alive forever, Caesar. I can only ensure you don't die today."

The winter brought news that made everything worse.

Rebellion in Judaea—more serious this time. The Jews had found a leader, Bar Kokhba, who claimed to be their messiah and was fighting with the desperation of people who had nothing left to lose. Cities burned. Legions marched. The eastern provinces trembled with uncertainty.

Hadrian received the reports in his private chambers, away from the courtiers and senators who might interpret weakness as opportunity. I was the only witness to his fury, his fear, his growing sense that the empire was unravelling faster than he could repair it.

"They're calling him the Son of the Star," he said, crumpling another dispatch. "Do you know what that means?"

"That they believe their god fights beside them."

"That they believe their god is stronger than mine." He struggled to his feet and moved to the window, where he could see smoke rising from the city below. Not rebellion smoke—just the ordinary fires of a winter evening. But in his current state, every shadow looked like a conspiracy. "Six years, Pythias. Six years, I've been building temples to Antinous, spreading his cult across the empire, proving that Roman gods can transform death into divinity. And what do I have to show for it?"

"Statues. Coins. Prayers."

"Marble and metal and empty words." His voice carried the bitterness of a man who had squandered his fortune on dreams. "The Jews believe their messiah will return from the dead to lead them to victory. I can't even make a dead boy answer my prayers."

I said nothing. What comfort could I offer? That the gods he invented were as real as any others? That faith built on lies was still faith? That love—even murderous love—might still count for something in whatever afterlife awaited emperors?

"More wine," he said.

I poured, tasted, and passed the cup. The ritual that had once been about poison had become something else—a moment of connection between two men who had shared too many secrets to pretend they were anything other than what they were.

"Do you ever think about your own death?" he asked.

"Every day. It's an occupational hazard."

"No, I mean, really think about it. What comes after? Whether there's anything beyond the last breath."

I considered the question while he drank. Did I believe in an afterlife? In gods who judged the living and the dead? In justice that transcended the boundaries of empire?

"I think the dead live on in the memory of those who loved them," I said at last.

"And those who had no one to love them?"

"They endure in the minds of those who witnessed them."

Hadrian nodded slowly. "Is that enough? Memory without monuments? Love without temples?"

"It's what most people get."

"But I'm not most people."

"No, Caesar. You're not."

He set down his cup and looked at me with something I had never seen in his eyes before. Not command. Not calculation. But something that might have been need.

"What will you remember about me, Pythias? When I'm gone and the Senate is deciding which of my acts deserve commemoration?"

The question hung between us like incense. I could have given him the expected answer—his buildings, his travels, his transformation of the empire from a collection of conquered territories into something resembling a civilisation. I could have mentioned his poetry, his philosophy, his genuine attempts to understand the people he ruled.

Instead, I told him the truth.

"I'll remember that you loved someone enough to destroy him."

Hadrian flinched as if I had struck him. "Is that how you see it? Destruction?"

"I see a boy who died afraid, and an emperor who convinced himself that murder was metamorphosis."

"And you've stayed with me anyway, all these years. Why?"

I had asked myself the same question countless times. Why hadn't I fled when I realised what truly happened by the Nile? Why had I continued to taste his wine, to listen to his midnight confessions, to enable his transformation of guilt into worship?

"Because someone needs to remember what really happened. And someone needs to ensure you live long enough to face what you've done."

"Face it, how?"

"That's not for me to decide, Caesar."

We sat in silence for a long time. Outside, the city settled into its evening rhythms—guards changing, taverns filling, families gathering around fires that would burn until dawn. The ordinary life of the empire continued regardless of the dramas played out in palace chambers.

"He appears to me sometimes," Hadrian said suddenly. "In dreams. Not the god-version—the boy. The one who used to ask about home."

"What does he say?"

"Nothing. He just looks at me. Not with anger, not with forgiveness. Just... recognition. As if he's waiting for me to understand something."

"Do you? Understand?"

Hadrian closed his eyes. In the lamplight, his face looked carved from wax—pale, fragile, already halfway to the tomb.

"I understand that I loved him more than I loved his life. More than I loved his happiness. More than I loved anything except my own need to possess what I could never truly have." He opened his eyes. "Does that make me a monster, Pythias?"

"It makes you human."

"I'm supposed to be more than human."

"Yes. That's the problem."

He laughed at that—a sound like autumn leaves rattling through empty courtyards.

"You're the only person left who tells me the truth," he said. "Do you know what that makes you?"

"Your taster."

"My only true mirror." His voice cracked slightly. "Everyone else reflects back what they think I want to see. You reflect what I am."

I had no answer for that. I had been trained to survive, not to be seen. To serve, not to matter. Yet somehow, in the space between tasting and trusting, between loyalty and honesty, I had become something I had never intended to be.

Essential.

"More wine, Caesar?"

"No. But stay. I don't want to face the dark alone."

So I stood by the wall, cup ready, watching an emperor confront the collapse of his immortality project. Outside, Rome dreamed of tomorrow's bread and tomorrow's circuses, unaware that in a palace chamber two men from the provinces were sharing the peculiar intimacy of those who had witnessed the unforgivable.

Some mirrors show you what you want to see.

Others show you what you are.

I had learned to be the second kind.

It was the most dangerous gift I could offer—and the only one he still needed.

CHAPTER 8:

MEMORY WITHOUT MONUMENTS

"The dead are never truly gone while the living remember their names."

— Cicero

Rome, 138 CE

They didn't wake me when he died.

I found out the way servants always do—through whispered conversations in corridors, through the sudden appearance of unfamiliar officials, through the particular quality of silence that settles over a household when its centre has stopped breathing.

I was in the kitchens, checking the morning wine that no one would drink, when Marcus appeared in the doorway. His face held the careful emptiness of a man delivering news that could reshape the world.

"It's finished," he said simply.

I set down my cup. "When?"

"Before dawn. Peaceful, they say. In his sleep."

Peaceful. I almost laughed. Nothing about Hadrian's last years had been peaceful. The war in Judaea had finally ended, but at a cost that haunted him. Bar Kokhba was dead, Jerusalem was rubble, and hundreds of thousands had perished for the privilege of calling their land by a different name. The emperor who had built walls to keep people out had spent his final months watching an entire province tear itself apart.

"Who else knows?"

"The praetorian prefect. The secretary of correspondence. They're preparing the announcements." Marcus lowered his voice. "There will be changes."

I understood. A new emperor meant new staff, new loyalties, new arrangements. People like us—those whose value depended entirely on the favour of the dead—would be evaluated, reassigned, or discarded according to the needs of the successor.

"Antoninus Pius," I said. It wasn't a question. Hadrian had been grooming his adopted heir for months, bringing him into audiences, consulting him on policy matters.

"Yes. He's already received the praetorian oath. Smooth transition." Marcus paused. "They say he's a practical man. Less given to... enthusiasms."

The word carried weight. Antoninus would not be building temples to dead boys or consulting Egyptian priests about divine transformations. He would focus on roads, laws, borders—the mundane work of empire that kept the world turning while emperors chased immortality.

"What about the household?"

"Most will stay. The new emperor needs continuity." Another pause. "Some positions may become... redundant."

I nodded. A food taster was only as valuable as the paranoia of the man he served. If Antoninus Pius felt secure enough to eat without fearing poison, my skills would be unnecessary.

"How long do I have?"

"They want an inventory of Hadrian's personal effects by evening. Papers, correspondence, private documents. The new administration wants to understand what they're inheriting."

I thought of the scrolls hidden beneath my sleeping mat—my own chronicle of the past eight years, written in careful Greek characters that recorded what no official history would ever acknowledge: the truth about Antinous, the reality behind the myths, the weight of watching power transform love into legend.

"I'll begin immediately," I said.

I went first to Hadrian's study, where he had spent his final months surrounded by architectural drawings and correspondence from across the empire. Morning light fell through windows he would never see again, illuminating papers covered in his increasingly shaky handwriting.

There were letters from provincial governors reporting on temple construction, requests for guidance on proper ritual observances, and updates on the progress of Antinoöpolis—the city that had grown around the spot where a boy had died and a god had been born.

I read them all, sorting them into categories that would make sense to Antoninus's administrators: state business here, personal correspondence there, theological matters in a separate pile that would likely be transferred to whatever priests inherited the management of imperial cult activities.

But it was the private papers that drew my attention—drafts of poems never completed, notes for memoirs never written, fragments of thought that revealed the mind behind the public face.

The Greeks were right about immortality. It is not about living forever; it is about being remembered perfectly. Death fixes you in amber, preserving you as you were in your best moment. The living continue to change, to disappoint, to grow old and strange. But the dead remain beautiful.

I think often of Alexander, who died at thirty-two with half the world still unconquered. Would we remember him so fondly if he had lived to sixty? If we had watched him grow cautious and calculating, making the small compromises survival requires?

Perhaps I loved Antinous because I knew he would never disappoint me. The dead are perfect because they can never be anything else.

I folded the papers carefully and placed them in the pile marked "Personal—Archive." Someone, someday, might try to understand Hadrian through these fragments. They would find self-awareness mixed with self-justification, insight tangled with delusion.

They would not find the full truth. That was hidden elsewhere, in scrolls that bore no imperial seal, written by a hand history had never learned to recognise.

By afternoon, the palace had filled with officials I did not recognise—men in senatorial togas conferring in hushed voices, secretaries carrying sealed documents between offices, the machinery of transition grinding into motion with the efficiency Rome was famous for.

I completed my inventory and delivered it to the chief secretary. Gaius was thin, precise—a man who had served three emperors and expected to serve a fourth. He glanced through my careful lists without really seeing them.

"Thorough work," he said absently. "The new administration appreciates competence."

"Thank you."

"There is one matter." He set down the papers and looked at me directly for the first time. "The Divine Hadrian's personal taster— that position will not be continued under Antoninus. Different security arrangements."

I had expected this, but hearing it spoken aloud still felt like a small death. For eight years, I had been essential. For eight years, my survival had been linked to an emperor's paranoia and need for absolute trust.

Now I was redundant.

"I understand," I said. "What arrangements are being made?"

"You'll receive a pension, of course—recognition of faithful service. And papers of formal manumission, should you wish to leave Rome entirely." He picked up a stylus and began making notes on a wax tablet. "Many former imperial servants retire to the provinces. They buy small farms, establish workshops, and live quietly on their savings."

"And if I prefer to remain in the city?"

"There are always positions for experienced household staff. Nothing as prestigious as imperial service, but comfortable situations with senatorial families or wealthy merchants." He looked up. "A recommendation from the imperial household carries considerable weight."

I thanked him and left, carrying papers that marked the end of one life and the beginning of another. In the space of a single conversation, I had been transformed from Pythias the imperial taster to Pythias the unemployed freedman, free to make choices I had never before been allowed to consider.

But freedom, I was discovering, was a more complicated gift than slavery.

That evening, I sat in my small chamber and considered my options. I could buy a farm in Bithynia, return to the province of my birth as a successful man made good by imperial service. I could remain in Rome and seek employment with a wealthy family, trading on my reputation and experience.

Or I could disappear entirely. Take a new name, travel to a distant city where no one knew my history, and start fresh as someone who had never tasted an emperor's wine or witnessed the creation of gods.

The third option appealed to me most. I was tired of being defined by my proximity to power, tired of being seen as an appendage to other people's stories. But I still had one task left to complete.

I pulled out my hidden chronicle—months of careful writing that documented what I had seen and heard during the final years of Hadrian's reign: the truth about Antinous, the reality behind the divine transformation, the weight of love that killed what it claimed to cherish.

Reading through my own words, I realised I had created something dangerous. Not because it revealed state secrets or military plans, but because it challenged the myths already hardening into official history. In ten, twenty, fifty years—when everyone who had known the living Antinous was dead—these scrolls might be the only record of who he truly was.

That made them valuable. It also made them lethal to anyone found possessing them.

I could burn them, as I had burned Hadrian's correspondence about Egyptian prophecies and star charts. I could hide them somewhere safe and hope they survived until someone who cared about the truth found them. Or I could take them with me, carrying the burden of memory until I found someone worthy of sharing it.

As I pondered these choices, a knock sounded at my door. I hid the scrolls quickly and opened them to find a young slave I didn't recognise.

"The new emperor wishes to see you," he said.

I followed him through corridors that looked the same but felt different, past guards who wore familiar armour but watched me with unfamiliar eyes. The palace was transforming itself around its new master, adapting to new needs and expectations.

Antoninus Pius received me in the same study where I had spent countless hours with Hadrian. But where his predecessor had filled the space with architectural models and letters from every corner of the empire, the new emperor had cleared everything away except for a single desk, three chairs, and a map of Italy on the wall.

"Pythias," he said, rising from behind the desk. He was younger than Hadrian, with the solid build of a man who had spent his career managing practical affairs rather than chasing philosophical abstractions. "I wanted to thank you personally for your service to my predecessor."

"It was my honour, Caesar."

"Eight years," he said, consulting a document on his desk. "Unprecedented loyalty in a position that requires... unique trust."

"The Divine Hadrian was generous with his confidence."

"Yes. I've been reading the household reports. It seems you were more than a food taster in the final years—companion, counsellor, keeper of private correspondence." He looked at me carefully. "Confidant."

The word lingered unspoken between us. I understood what he was really asking: how much did I know? How many secrets had I accumulated? How dangerous was it to let me walk away with Hadrian's private conversations still fresh in my memory?

"I served in whatever capacity the emperor required," I said carefully.

"I'm sure you did." Antoninus moved to the window and looked out over the city that was now his to govern. "The thing about confidants is that they know things. Personal things. Private conversations that might be misunderstood if they became public knowledge."

"I was trained for discretion, Caesar."

"I'm sure you were. But training and practice are different things." He turned back to me. "Tell me, Pythias—what do you remember about the Divine Antinous?"

The question was a trap, carefully baited. I could give him the official version—divine youth, willing sacrifice, glorious transformation. Or I could hint at darker knowledge, suggest that I knew things that might complicate the mythology his predecessor had worked so hard to establish.

Either answer would mark me as dangerous.

"I remember that the Divine Hadrian loved him," I said at last. "Everything else is theology, which is above my understanding."

Antoninus smiled—not with warmth, but with the satisfaction of a man who had received the answer he expected.

"Wise response. Theology should indeed be left to theologians." He returned to his desk and picked up another document.

"I have a proposition for you, Pythias. A final service to the imperial household."

"Caesar?"

"There's a villa in Campania. Modest but comfortable, with vineyards and olive groves. Good income, peaceful location, far enough from Rome to ensure... tranquillity." He set down the paper. "It could be yours, with a generous pension, in exchange for your agreement to live quietly. Very quietly."

I understood. This wasn't retirement—it was exile. Comfortable exile, well-compensated exile, but exile nonetheless. The price of knowing too much and living too long.

"And if I decline this generous offer?"

"Then you would remain in Rome, of course. Free to seek employment wherever you choose. Though I suspect you might find the competition... challenging. Former imperial servants sometimes discover that their skills are less transferable than they had hoped."

The threat was politely delivered but unmistakable: accept exile, or face slow starvation in a city where no one would dare employ someone the new emperor had marked as untrustworthy.

"The villa sounds pleasant," I said.

"Excellent. The papers will be ready tomorrow. You can depart whenever you find it convenient."

I was dismissed with the same efficiency that had marked the entire transition. No ceremony, no formal recognition of service—just the quiet disposal of a problem that could complicate the new administration's efforts to distance itself from its predecessor's more exotic enthusiasms.

I returned to my chamber and completed my packing. The possessions I had accumulated over eight years of imperial service fit easily into two travelling cases: clothes, a few books, and some small personal items of no particular value.

And hidden among them, protected by waxed linen, were the scrolls containing the only honest account of the past decade's events—the truth about Antinous. The truth the empire could not bear to let live and longed to strangle into silence.

I would take them to Campania, to a villa sufficiently distant from Rome to guarantee peace. I would tend grapes and olives and live quietly, as promised.

But I would also write. Complete the chronicle. Tell the full story while memory remains fresh and details stay sharp.

And someday, when I was old enough to stop caring about consequences, I would find someone to entrust with the truth.

Not because I expected justice—the dead were beyond help, and the guilty were beyond reach.

But because someone should know. Someone should remember. Someone should taste the real vintage beneath all the sweet myths poured out for public consumption.

The villa was indeed modest, pleasant, and quiet. But the silence was deeper than Antoninus had intended.

It was the silence of a witness, biding its time for the right moment to speak.

CHAPTER 9:

THE HOUSE OF DUST

"Truth is like wine: it improves with age, but few have the stomach for the vintage."

— Roman saying

Campania, 151 CE

Twenty years of silence had taught me that truth ferments differently than wine.

The villa sat on a hillside overlooking the Bay of Naples, where fishing boats moved like prayers across waters that reflected only sky. I had grown comfortable with exile, marking seasons by grape harvests rather than imperial audiences, measuring time by the slow accumulation of honest calluses on hands that had once known only the weight of silver cups.

My neighbours knew me as Marcus Pythias—a retired freedman who had served in some minor capacity in Rome, prosperous enough to own land but humble enough to work it himself. I bought their produce, hired their sons during harvest season, and attended their festivals without drawing attention. The perfect disappeared man.

But truth has a way of finding you, even when you've spent decades learning to hide from it.

The visitors arrived on a morning when the sea ran silver and the wind carried no memories. I was in my olive grove, checking the press that had been giving me trouble all week, when I heard cart wheels grinding against stone and saw the dust cloud that meant strangers were coming with purpose.

Three men. The leader dismounted with the careful grace of someone whose hands had never known honest work—soft palms, manicured nails, the kind of deliberately casual dress that cost more than most people earned in a month. His companions stayed with the cart, but their eyes swept my property with the professional assessment of men who knew how to catalogue wealth and weakness in equal measure.

"Marcus Pythias?"

"I am."

"Gaius Tranquillus. I'm writing a biography of the Caesars—the lives of the emperors from Julius through Domitian." He paused, studying my face for some reaction I was careful not to give. "I believe you served the Divine Hadrian?"

Twenty years collapsed into heartbeats. The olive grove around me seemed to shimmer, and for a moment I was back in marble corridors, testing wine for poison that never came, listening to midnight conversations that revealed the darkest corners of imperial love.

"I did," I said carefully.

"For eight years, including his final period, when his health declined. Including the journey to Egypt, when the Divine Antinous achieved transformation."

The formal phrasing didn't hide what he was really asking. I gestured toward my villa. "Would you care for some refreshment? The morning is growing warm."

I led them into my receiving room—simple furniture, local pottery, nothing that suggested I had once moved through the halls of power. The wine I poured came from grapes that had never been tested for poison, never been tasted by trembling lips that counted each breath as borrowed time.

"You have a beautiful property," Tranquillus said, accepting his cup. "Peaceful. Far from the complications of city life."

"That was the intention."

He pulled out a wax tablet covered in neat lines of writing. "I've been granted access to the imperial archives for my research. The records are comprehensive—temples, festivals, treatises. Yet every scroll tells the same story, too polished, as if edited by one hand."

I waited.

"But I've spoken to other former servants—kitchen staff who prepared meals for the Egyptian journey, guards who were present during the search for the body, sailors who worked the Nile barges." He looked up from his tablet. "Their stories have... variations. Small inconsistencies that suggest the official version may be incomplete."

A gust of wind stirred the olive trees outside my window. Twenty years of Mediterranean sun had weathered their leaves to silver, but their roots ran deep enough to withstand any storm. I had learned something about survival from watching them.

"What did you see, Pythias?"

The uncertainty separated us like a dense fog.

"I saw an emperor who loved deeply," I said at last.

"And?"

"And love is not always gentle."

Tranquillus set down his wine cup. The sound seemed unnaturally loud in the quiet room. "Do you give me history—or myth?"

"I hope to write truth."

"Truth has consequences. For the living and the dead."

"I'm aware of that." I moved to the window, where I could see my workers tending the vines in the distance. "Truth is a dangerous vintage. Most people prefer the sweet lies they're used to drinking. Truth lingers with a bitter aftertaste."

"Then the archives lie?"

"The archives are incomplete. Like wine that's been watered down—still recognisable, but missing the elements that give it strength. Still nourishing, but not the vintage that was actually pressed."

I studied the three faces watching me—men who had travelled from Rome seeking stories to fill the gaps in imperial records. After twenty years of tending vines and pressing olives, of living as an invisible man in an invisible corner of the empire, I found myself at the centre of history again.

"The Divine Antinous is worshipped across the empire," I said. "Thousands have found meaning in his story. Pilgrims travel to Egypt to visit the spot where a god was born. Artists carve his face in marble, poets compose hymns in his honour. Would you destroy their faith for the sake of historical accuracy?"

"Would you preserve lies for the sake of comfortable ignorance?"

The question cut deeper than he probably intended. For twenty years, I had preserved the most dangerous lies—not through repetition, but through silence. Every sunrise I did not speak was another day that comfortable myths could flourish unchallenged.

"What guarantees do I have that anything I tell you won't result in my quiet disappearance from this villa? I've grown fond of breathing. It's become something of a habit."

"Antoninus is dead. Marcus Aurelius rules now, and he cares more about philosophical consistency than protecting uncomfortable inheritances from previous reigns." Tranquillus leaned forward slightly. "Besides, someone, somewhere, always knows what really happened. The question is whether that knowledge serves any purpose by remaining hidden."

I went to my bedroom and retrieved the scrolls I had spent twenty years perfecting—adding details as memory sharpened them, revising passages as understanding deepened. The chronicle felt heavier than papyrus should, weighted with accumulated secrets that had nearly killed me to preserve.

When I returned to the receiving room, I placed them on the table beside the official documents his companions had spread out like battle plans.

"This contains what I witnessed," I said. "Written by someone who was there for every cup of wine, every midnight conversation, every decision that transformed a boy from Bithynia into a god worshipped across the empire."

Tranquillus reached for the nearest scroll.

"One condition," I said, keeping my hand on it. "You read it completely or not at all. No cherry-picking comfortable truths while ignoring the ugly ones. If you want to know what really happened, you must accept all of what really happened."

"Agreed."

I let him take the scroll. As he began to read, I watched his face change. The academic certainty of someone gathering information for a scholarly project gradually gave way to something more complex—recognition, perhaps, of the weight that truth carries when it is finally spoken aloud.

They never poisoned Hadrian. Even if they had tried, I would have noticed. That was my role. For eight years, I stood beside him while he loved a boy deeply enough to kill him—while he grieved deeply enough to make that murder holy.

"You were there for all of this?" he asked after reading several passages.

"Every word. Every cup of wine. Every decision."

He continued reading while his companions compared my private account with the official version that had shaped the empire's understanding of its strangest love story. The silence stretched between us, broken only by the rustle of papyrus and the distant sound of my workers finishing their daily tasks.

"The prophecy," Tranquillus said suddenly. "The Egyptian priests who spoke of divine sacrifice. You're saying it was arranged?"

"I'm saying Hadrian consulted with Egyptian theologians for months before the journey. The 'ancient prophecy' was commissioned to provide religious justification for what he had already decided to do."

"And Antinous knew?"

Antinous suspected. But suspicion isn't knowledge, and knowledge isn't power. He was nineteen years old, isolated from everything familiar, completely dependent on the favour of a man who had convinced himself that love required sacrifice."

Tranquillus set down the scroll and glanced at me with something that might have been horror. "You speak of murder."

"I'm describing transformation. "The physical transformation of a living boy into a dead god. The political conversion of personal obsession into imperial policy. The historical reshaping of an ugly truth into a beautiful lie." I refilled our wine cups, performing the ritual of tasting that had defined my life for so many years. "All transformations require something to die."

"If I write this, it will destroy the cult of Antinous. People will learn that their god was once human, that his sacrifice was not willing—"

"Truth unmasks myth. Some will rejoice, some despair. Most will shrug and keep living." I gestured toward the window, where farmers were bringing in their harvest under an indifferent sun. "The world has a remarkable capacity for continuing regardless of what intellectuals write about dead emperors."

"Which serves Rome better?"

The question surprised me with its honesty. After decades of dancing around dangerous truths, here was someone willing to acknowledge that historical accuracy and political utility might not always align.

"The lie serves Rome better," I said. "It gives people something to worship, something to aspire to, something to believe in that transcends the brutal realities of power. The truth serves truth better. But truth and empire are not natural allies."

"Then why are you giving this to me?"

I thought of Antinous as I had last seen him—not the marble statues that captured his beauty in eternal youth, but the frightened boy standing at a barge's rail, asking questions about dreams and death while the Nile flowed beneath him toward an uncertain delta.

"Because he was real—he laughed, he missed his father's tavern, he cried when he thought no one watched. Turning him into a symbol erases the human boy. Someone should remember what truly happened beneath the sweet myths."

"And if I choose to suppress it? File it away in some archive where it will gather dust until the empire falls?"

"Then you choose to suppress it. I've done my part. I've preserved the testimony. What you do with it is between you and your conscience."

The afternoon had grown late while we talked. Golden light slanted through my windows, transforming the simple room into something that might have been beautiful—if beauty were measured by the quality of illumination rather than the cost of decoration.

"I need time to think," Tranquillus said at last.

"Take all the time you need. The truth isn't going anywhere."

As they prepared to leave, he gathered the scrolls carefully, wrapping them in oiled cloth as if they were something precious and fragile. Which, in their way, they were.

"Why now?" he asked as his companions loaded their cart. "You could have taken this secret to your grave. Why speak now?"

I considered the question while evening settled over the Bay of Naples. Somewhere in the distance, a fisherman sang as he brought his boat home to harbour. The song was older than Rome, older than emperors and their beautiful boys, older than the need to transform murder into mythology.

"Because I'm tired of being the only one who remembers," I said. "Memory shared is memory preserved. Memory hoarded is just another form of burial."

After they left, I sat alone in my receiving room, listening to the familiar sounds of evening in the countryside. My workers had gone home to their families. My neighbours were preparing simple meals and sharing the small gossip that made ordinary life possible.

For twenty years, I had lived among them without quite belonging, carrying secrets meaningless to their lives but vital to the histories inked in distant archives. Now those secrets were no longer mine alone.

I felt lighter. The burden of silence, carried so long I had forgotten its weight, was lifted. Whatever happened next would happen without my participation.

I had done what I was trained to do: taste poison, survive, and pass warning. What they chose to do with that warning was no longer my responsibility.

That night, I slept better than I had in years. No dreams of marble boys, grieving emperors, or the taste of wine laced with unspoken guilt. Just the peaceful darkness of someone who had completed a task borne longer than memory itself.

I had tasted the vintage of truth, found it bitter but necessary, and passed the cup to someone else.

My silence was broken. My duty was done.

EPILOGUE:

THE BIOGRAPHER'S CHOICE

Rome, 152 CE

Tranquillus never published the complete truth about Antinous.

In Lives of the Caesars, he mentioned the beautiful boy who died in Egypt, the grief-stricken emperor who deified him, the temples and festivals that preserved his memory. Yet the account maintained the mystery rather than solving it, hinting at complexities without revealing their full extent.

Perhaps he thought the empire wasn't ready for the truth. Perhaps he thought the truth wasn't ready for the empire. Or perhaps he simply chose comfort over courage, as most people do when history forces them to choose between what is useful and what is honest.

The scrolls disappeared into the imperial archives, filed away with thousands of other documents recording the small daily details of administrative life. The truth became another bureaucratic entry—preserved but forgotten—available to anyone who cared enough to look, yet invisible to anyone who preferred not to see.

Still, the cult of Antinous flourished. Temples rose in cities across the Mediterranean. Artists carved his face in marble, his features growing more beautiful with each new rendering. Poets composed hymns in his honour, praising divine love over human frailty. Priests developed elaborate mysteries to explain his transformation from mortal beauty to divine presence.

And in a villa overlooking the Bay of Naples, an old man tended his vines and watched the seasons turn, knowing that somewhere in the imperial archives, wrapped in oiled cloth and sealed with wax, the truth waited patiently for someone brave enough to taste it.

Some poisons take generations to work their way through the system. Some truths are worth preserving even when they are too dangerous to speak. And some silences, once broken, echo forward through centuries, waiting for the right moment to be heard.

The taster's duty was never just to detect poison in the present. It was to preserve the possibility of recognition for a future wise enough to handle truth without dying from it.

That possibility, at least, remained. And that possibility would have to be enough.

AUTHOR'S NOTE

These stories began with fragments—hostile mentions in ancient texts, archaeological shadows, the silences between what was recorded and what was lived.

Sporus appears in three lines of Suetonius. Hierocles survives in Cassius Dio's sneer as evidence of depravity. Pythias does not appear in the record at all—I found him in the margins, in the necessity of every emperor's need for someone to taste his wine.

I did not write these novellas to reclaim them as heroes or martyrs, but to imagine them as people. Ancient sources saw them only through the lens of scandal and judgement. Yet scandal always begins with human beings, not symbols.

The scaffolding of these stories is history: ceremonies, households, crises reconstructed from evidence. But their inner lives—their thoughts, fears, and strategies for survival—those I had to imagine. I tried to imagine with both rigour and empathy.

The Rome in these pages is a world of constant transformation: political, religious, bodily, psychological. Identity was performance, and performance was survival. Power flowed like water, filling every void, reshaping everything it touched.

Some were consumed by this system. Others learned to navigate it. A few preserved something essential while adapting everything else.

Sporus, Hierocles, Pythias—each found a strategy. None emerged unchanged. All remained human.

That, in the end, may be the only victory that matters.

HISTORICAL NOTES

Elagabalus and Hierocles

Elagabalus (203–222 CE), born in Emesa, Syria, became emperor at fourteen through a coup engineered by his grandmother, Julia Maesa. As hereditary high priest of the sun god Elagabal, he brought foreign rites to Rome, erecting a temple on the Palatine Hill and proclaiming his god supreme over Jupiter.

Ancient sources describe Elagabalus adopting female titles and seeking bodily alteration—accounts that suggest a gender expression outside Roman norms. While modern categories such as "transgender" cannot be applied directly, their self-presentation unsettled Roman masculinity and remains strikingly ambiguous.

Cassius Dio records that Elagabalus called himself the "mistress, wife, and queen of Hierocles," a charioteer from the provinces whose fame came through the racetrack. For Rome, his ascent from circus to imperial bed was scandalous, crossing lines of class, decorum, and gender all at once.

The historical record offers only fragments. This book imagines Hierocles's backstory, his emotional journey, and the possibility of exile as his chosen end—a silence filled with plausible invention.

Nero and Sporus

Nero (37–68 CE) became emperor at sixteen and ruled for fourteen turbulent years. Guided at first by advisors, he descended into artistic obsession and excess until rebellion forced his suicide.

One of the darkest episodes of his reign involved Sporus, a provincial youth whom Nero reportedly had castrated and married, dressed as the dead empress Poppaea, and paraded in public as "Augusta." Ancient sources tell the story with cruelty; none grant Sporus an inner life.

After Nero's death, Sporus was used as a pawn by rivals in the Year of Four Emperors, until he chose suicide over public execution. History reduces him to a grotesque symbol of imperial decadence. This book reimagines him as a person: enduring an identity imposed by power, carving out moments of agency where he could, and claiming his ending on his own terms.

Hadrian and Pythias

Hadrian (76–138 CE) ruled for two decades at the empire's height. A passionate Hellenophile, he built cities, monuments, and a cult of Greek culture across the empire.

His defining relationship was with Antinous, the Bithynian youth who drowned in the Nile in 130 CE. Hadrian's grief reshaped Rome: he founded Antinoöpolis, declared Antinous a god, raised temples, and filled the empire with statues of the boy. Ancient sources focus on the spectacle. None considers the practical work of transforming grief into religion.

Who managed the rituals? Who shielded the emperor from poison and plot when he was most vulnerable?

Food tasters were essential to every imperial household: invisible servants whose task was to detect danger at the table while overhearing the conversations of power. Their role demanded intelligence, discretion, and loyalty.

Pythias, in this book, represents that hidden figure: the witness who preserved truth while remaining unrecorded. His name is borrowed from a maidservant of Octavia, Nero's first wife, who defied Tigellinus under torture. Recast here as Hadrian's food taster, Pythias carries forward the same courage in a different setting. He stands for all those who served in silence yet held the power of witness.

Notes on Historical Interpretation

The ancient sources on Nero and Elagabalus are hostile, written by senatorial historians who despised both rulers. Tacitus, Suetonius, Cassius Dio, and the Historia Augusta shaped narratives steeped in moral judgement. Their reliability is uneven, their biases obvious.

Modern scholarship reads these texts critically, using comparative evidence, archaeology, and anthropology to reconstruct the lives behind polemic. In writing these novellas, I drew on:

Prosopography to trace individuals across fragmentary mentions

Archaeology to ground daily life in material evidence

Anthropology to illuminate gender roles and survival strategies under oppression

The past does not map cleanly onto the present. Roman sexuality was structured around penetration and status, not orientation. Gender variance was often tied to cult and ritual, not identity. Survival under an empire required compromises foreign to modern ideals of authenticity.

These stories honour ancient complexity without forcing modern definitions onto it. They imagine possibilities within silence, while acknowledging the limits of what we can know.

ACKNOWLEDGMENTS

This book rests on the work of scholars who have devoted their lives to illuminating the lives of people ancient texts tried to erase. Any errors here are my own; the foundation is theirs.

I am indebted to those who study Roman slavery, households, and daily life—to those who search for the silenced voices beneath the din of senatorial disdain.

I also owe gratitude to contemporary survivors whose testimonies of resilience and trauma informed my imagination of what it means to preserve dignity under dehumanising systems. Though the contexts differ, the questions are eternal.

Finally, I dedicate these pages to all who were consumed by empire, and to the fragments of themselves they managed to preserve. Their endurance matters not as symbols, but as proof of humanity's refusal to vanish.

That may be the most important story of all.

BIBLIOGRAPHY AND FURTHER READING

Primary Sources

Cassius Dio, Roman History (Loeb Classical Library)

Suetonius, Lives of the Caesars

Tacitus, Annals and Histories

Historia Augusta, "Life of Elagabalus"

Herodian, History of the Empire

Modern Scholarship

Champlin, Edward. Nero (Harvard, 2003)

Griffin, Miriam. Nero: The End of a Dynasty (Yale, 1984)

De Arrizabalaga y Prado, Leonardo. The Emperor Elagabalus: Fact or Fiction? (Wisconsin, 2010)

Beard, Mary. SPQR: A History of Ancient Rome (Liveright, 2015)

Williams, Craig. Roman Homosexuality (2nd ed., OUP, 2010)

Hallett, Judith & Skinner, Marilyn, eds. Roman Sexualities (Princeton, 1997)

Bradley, Keith. Slaves and Masters in the Roman Empire (OUP, 1987)
Joshel, Sandra. Slavery in the Roman World (CUP, 2010)

READING GUIDE

For book clubs, classrooms, and discussion:

1. Identity and Transformation → How does each protagonist maintain selfhood while adapting to survive?
2. Power and Agency → What choices remain when every structure is designed to deny them?
3. Narrative Voice → How does memory years later shape the telling of each story?
4. History and Imagination → What can fiction reveal about the past that history cannot?
5. Contemporary Resonance → Without imposing modern categories, what echoes of today can be found in these ancient struggles?

ABOUT THE AUTHOR

J. H. M. Carlisle is a pen name. The author writes historical and political fiction drawing from contemporary events, and prefers to maintain their privacy.

ABOUT THE PUBLISHER

RONDANINI PUBLISHING™ LTD

Rondanini Publishing™ was founded by Luigi Pascal Rondanini, a published author in Italy who experienced firsthand the challenges that writers face in today's publishing landscape. After witnessing talented authors being asked to buy their own work and shoulder marketing responsibilities, Luigi recognised that the industry too often prioritises profit over partnership.

OUR MISSION

We believe in genuine partnership built on respect for the author's craft and investment in their success. Authors are never required to purchase their own copies or contribute financially to production costs. If we believe in your work enough to publish it, we invest in its success.

WHAT WE PUBLISH

From compelling historical fiction to thought-provoking literary works, we champion diverse voices and innovative storytelling. Our catalogue includes fiction, non-fiction excellence, short story collections, and educational resources that serve both professional and general audiences.

INTERNATIONAL REACH

Operating in both English and Italian markets, we bring a global perspective to publishing while maintaining deep roots in literary tradition. Our bilingual approach opens doors for authors seeking to reach diverse audiences across cultural and linguistic boundaries.

OUR COMMITMENT

Rondanini Publishing™ Ltd exists to serve literature and the authors who create it. We measure success not just in sales figures, but in the careers we help build and the stories we help share with the world.

For more information: **www.rondanini.com**

For authors seeking a publisher who values craft over commerce and partnership over profit.

www.ingramcontent.com/pod-product-compliance
Ingram Content Group UK Ltd.
Pitfield, Milton Keynes, MK11 3LW, UK
UKHW041908140925
462902UK00004B/123

9 781918 177008